Please renew or return items by the date shown on your receipt.

www.hertfordshire.gov.uk/libraries

Renewals and enquiries: 0300 123 4049

Textphone for hearing or 0300 123 4041
speech impaired users:

L32 11.16

maybe a Fox

Kathi Appelt and Alison McGhee

WALKER
BOOKS

First published in Great Britain 2016 by Walker Books Ltd
87 Vauxhall Walk, London SE11 5HJ

2 4 6 8 10 9 7 5 3 1

Text © 2016 Kathi Appelt and Alison McGhee
Cover art © 2016 Róbert Farkas

The right of Kathi Appelt and Alison McGhee to be identified as
authors of this work has been asserted by them in accordance with
the Copyright, Designs and Patents Act 1988

This book has been typeset in Joanna

Printed and bound in Great Britain by Clays Ltd, St Ives plc

British Library Cataloguing in Publication Data:
a catalogue record for this book is available from the British Library

ISBN 978-1-4063-7289-2

www.walker.co.uk

For M.T. Anderson, Nicole Griffin and
Marion Dane Bauer, with love

SHOULD THE FOX COME AGAIN
TO MY CABIN IN THE SNOW

Then, the winter will have fallen all in white
and the hill will be rising to the north,
the night also rising and leaving,
dawn light just coming in, the fire out.

Down the hill running will come that flame
among the dancing skeletons of the ash trees.
I will leave the door open for him.

Patricia Fargnoli

From under her covers, Jules Sherman listened for her sister, Sylvie, to walk out of their room. As soon as she did, Jules slipped out of bed and slammed the door behind her. She was still angry. Who did Sylvie think she was? The day before, Sylvie had once again left her at the bottom of the front porch steps and run into the woods, disappeared, her wavy red-brown hair swishing down her back, ignoring Jules's pleas to wait up, for once just *wait up*.

Sylvie was *always* doing that. Taking off. So fast. Time after time, leaving Jules standing there. Alone.

Jules's cheeks flushed with a bright blaze of anger. Here she was standing alone again, this time in the echo of the slammed bedroom door. The morning was still early. A grey dimness came in through their window, aided only by a thin beam from the hallway that slipped in under the door.

Even in the shallow light Jules could still see Sylvie's favourite T-shirt, along with the sweater and jeans Sylvie planned to wear that day, all laid out on her sister's bed. Jules hesitated, then grabbed the T-shirt, went straight to the windowsill and, in one swift motion, swept all her rocks into it, using it as a kind of basket. Ha! Sylvie would hate that. Her precious, precious T-shirt.

It was thin and soft and smelled like cotton and coconut shampoo and Sylvie. Jules took a deep breath. Sylvie loved coconut shampoo. In fact, she loved anything that smelled like coconut – coconut ice cream, coconut candy, coconut candles, including the one Sam had given her for Christmas. Sylvie said coconut was her "signature scent".

Jules wondered what her own signature scent was. One thing for sure, it wasn't coconut.

She dumped the rocks onto her bed and then did the same thing with the rocks from her bookcase, the rocks on top of her dresser and the rocks from the wooden box her dad had made her for Christmas. The rocks spilled across the mountains and valleys of her sheets and blanket. She tossed her pillow aside and scooped the rocks into the empty space left by the missing pillow.

Jules pulled the tiny hand lens that she wore on a lanyard around her neck out from under her pyjama top. Her dad had only recently given it to her. The lens was about the size of a quarter, and a bright LED light shone out from it.

"Every rock hound should have one," Dad had told her.

The lens magnified everything by ten times. When Jules held it against the surface of the rocks, she could see the striations where the different elements had folded into one another, or the smooth, shiny edges where the rock had been either chiselled by a pick or broken apart by some bigger force, maybe a glacier, as if the rock had been rubbed smooth by thousands of tonnes of sliding ice.

Not for the first time, her small LED light felt like a miniature sun, shining down on her own constellation of rock planets. Her bed was the galaxy, the Sherman Galaxy, bounded only by sheets and a warm fleece blanket.

Now she could begin to sort the rocks. First into the three categories: igneous, sedimentary and metamorphic. Then by size within each category. Then into vertical rows, horizontal rows and circles. As she sorted and arranged, she felt herself growing calmer. She whispered their

names aloud as she worked: "*Marble. Slate. Schist.*
Quartzite. Sandstone. Flint. Dolomite."

There was a fourth category of rocks too, one
that didn't have a scientific name. Wish rocks.
Rocks for the river. These were rocks that she
didn't display. Instead she kept them in an old
striped sock that had once belonged to Dad. It
was tucked in the back of hers and Sylvie's closet,
next to their shoes and boots.

Most of the wish rocks she had found herself,
either by spotting them along the trail or, lately,
with the help of her special pick hammer, an
Estwing E13P. It had taken her for ever to save
enough to buy the hammer, and even then it
had to be specially ordered by Mrs Bowen at
the Hobbston Hardware Store in town. Not only
that, but Dad wouldn't let her buy it without also
buying a pair of safety goggles.

"You want to be safe, don't you, Jules?" Sylvie
had asked her. Of course she did, and besides,

no true rock hound would be caught chipping away at rocks without a pair of safety goggles. Jules knew that. But it was hard to wait until she had enough money for both the hammer and the goggles. And then Sylvie did something surprising – she let Jules borrow the additional ten dollars so she wouldn't have to wait any longer to order the hammer. Sylvie was always doing stuff like that.

Remembering the goggles made Jules feel a little less angry with Sylvie. But not completely. She was still sick of being left behind. She snapped the beam of light off and tucked the lens back under her pyjama top.

She concentrated on her rocks, the ones spread before her in neat rows on her bed, and reached for one of her very favourites from the entire collection. Her fingers first hesitated over the small chunk of dark green-black marble. Then she remembered that Sylvie had brought that one back for her from a school field trip to the Danby marble quarry. Marble, slate and granite were the official state rocks of Vermont, where they lived. Jules loved that piece of marble, its cool smoothness. She loved to press it against her cheek.

But not this morning. She wouldn't choose the marble today. Not when she was angry at Sylvie. Instead she chose the piece of blue-grey slate that she herself had found at the edge of the Whippoorwill River, the river that ran along the edge of their property. She pressed her fingertips against its sharp edge. This would be a good skipping rock. Not that she would ever dream of sending it away across the water, never to be seen again. There were rocks for the river and rocks for the Sherman Galaxy. This one was a keeper, a blue-grey slate planet.

"Knock-knock!"

Sylvie, outside the door. She never knocked

with her hand, just her voice. Who did that? Right now Sylvie's voice-knock bugged Jules as much as being left in the dust.

"Go away."

"I can't. This is my room too, remember? And I have to get dressed."

Oops. The T-shirt! Sylvie's precious Flo-Jo T-shirt. Flo-Jo was Sylvie's hero, Florence Griffith-Joyner. She held the record for the fastest women's hundred-metre sprint in history, and Jules knew that Sylvie dreamed of beating that record. She also knew that was one of the reasons that Sylvie was always running. But knowing it didn't make it any easier. Sometimes Jules felt like the only side she ever saw of Sylvie was her back, growing smaller and smaller as she shot down the track or the trail or wherever else she ran. Jules smoothed out the T-shirt as best she could and returned it to its spot on Sylvie's bed. Sylvie always made her bed and laid out her clothes the second she got up. Unlike Jules, whose bed was always a mess. Especially messy when she did a major sorting of rocks. Like now.

"Knock-knock," came Sylvie's voice again. "Come on, Jules, let me in."

"There's no lock," Jules called. "Duh."

There had never been a lock on their door. Even though she was upset, Jules still had to admire that Sylvie hadn't just barged right in the way she, Jules, might have done. The doorknob turned and there was Sylvie, tall and skinny in her pyjamas. She got straight to the point.

"Why are you mad?"

"I'm not," Jules lied.

Sylvie just pointed at the rocks laid out on Jules's bed, a sure sign that Jules was trying to calm herself down.

"Come on. Tell me. I'm your one and only sister."

"Stop."

"What? I am, aren't I? Unless you've got a secret other sister somewhere?"

Sylvie sat down on Jules's bed, careful not to disturb the rocks. Then she sidled her pointer finger bit by bit, like a snake, through the rumpled blankets toward Jules. She had been doing that ever since they were tiny, and it always made Jules laugh. Jules looked away so she wouldn't start to soften.

Sylvie abandoned the finger-snake and instead picked up the one piece of obsidian in Jules's collection. She hefted the small polished oval in her hand.

"I remember when Mom gave you this," she said. "It was your fourth birthday. You were already crazy about rocks." She rolled her eyes in a what-a-weird-little-kid-you-were kind of way. "Seriously, what four-year-old kid is a rock fiend?"

That was it! Jules snatched the obsidian from

Sylvie's hand. Once again, Sylvie had invoked Mom. Obsidian was caused by volcanoes, an eruption of steam and gas so furious that it melted the earth itself into this hard, shiny object. Right then, Jules felt hard and shiny.

"You and Dad," she said. "You're like a secret club."

"What are you talking about?"

"When the two of you get going about Mom. How do you think it makes me feel?"

Sylvie looked puzzled. Jules kept going. "It's like you remember everything about her!" Jules rubbed her thumb along the smooth surface of the obsidian. "But me? I hardly remember anything. All I see when I try to picture her is her hair, which is exactly like ... like..."

She stopped talking and carefully placed the obsidian back on her bed, back into the vertical category of igneous rocks.

"Mine," Sylvie finished the sentence. "The

same colour as mine. Is that what you were going to say?"

Jules nodded. Yes. That was what she was going to say.

What she wasn't going to say: that no matter how hard she tried, her memories of their mom grew smaller and smaller, each one folding in on itself, so that not even her 10x magnifier could see them.

"I guess I do look like Mom," Sylvie said. "But you look like Dad. That makes us even. Right?"

Jules peered down at the Sherman Galaxy spread out on her bed. Once sorted into rows, the chaotic galaxy grew smaller and more orderly. The piece of blue-grey slate was still in her hand. That it wasn't the chunk of marble that Sylvie had given her felt like a tiny rebellion, not that Sylvie would ever know. Which was fine with Jules. Sisters didn't have to know everything about each other, right? Sylvie started to sneak her finger across the blanket again, trying to make Jules laugh. Sylvie hated any discord, even momentary, between the two of them. *It's you and me, sister,* she always said. *We've got each other's backs.* Then something caught Sylvie's eye, something outside the window.

"Hey! It's snowing!"

"Snow?" said Jules. "For real?"

She slid off the bed and stepped next to Sylvie. Through the panes of glass she could see it, big fat flakes tumbling from the sky. And from the looks of it, there were already a few centimetres covering the ground. Sylvie started hopping from one foot to the other. Jules felt a thin sliver of joy making its way into the frosty air between them.

"If we hurry, we have time to make one more snow family," said Sylvie. "Quick, grab your boots!"

Jules and Sylvie were all about their snow families, tiny snow sculptures that they made whenever the snow was new. Jules placed the blue-grey piece of slate back on her bed instead of returning it to the row of other metamorphic rocks. She liked thinking about it as a planet, at least for now. Her rocks and her frustration could wait.

"Hurry!" Sylvie said, pulling her hoodie and mittens on right over her PJs.

"Coming," said Jules. Her annoyance slipped away. She pulled on her own hoodie and mittens and followed her sister to the mudroom, where they yanked on their boots. Jules barely had hers on when Sylvie grabbed her hand and pulled her through the kitchen door. Together they jumped off the steps of the front porch. Two sisters, still in their flannel pyjamas, flying through the crisp air.

Slow and fast. Thick and thin. Eleven and twelve. Jules and Sylvie. *Thick as thieves,* their dad called them. *You and me, sister,* Sylvie always said. Which just now was entirely true. They were snowbirds, snow girls, snow sisters. Now all of

Jules's irritation vanished in the cold, clean smell of new snow.

"Perfect packing snow," Sylvie said, but Jules could already tell that by the way her boots sank into it, making a solid footprint. "Let's get started."

The falling flakes looked like snow moths. Jules cupped her hands and caught one. It lingered, then melted into her blue mittens. She took a deep breath. It was a gift from the sky, this snow, when they'd thought the last snow was ... well ... the *last*. With the days beginning to get longer and warmer, Jules had believed that their chances of new snow were done. No more tiny snow families tucked about the house – next to the porch, under the big maple, circling the mailbox. But now, here it was.

And here she was, in her PJs and boots, snow moths settling all around them in a thickening layer.

"Where should we put this family?" said Jules, turning in a circle.

The other, older snow families scattered about were mostly half-melted, their misshapen snow bodies leaning toward the earth, more ice than snow. In fact, Jules could feel the thin layer of ice underneath her boots, the result of thawing days and freezing nights. It made a fantastic crackling sound as she walked.

"How about by the beginning of the Slip trail?" said Sylvie, pointing toward the narrow footpath that led through the woods to the river. "There's room there."

Jules sucked in the cold air. Shivered. "OK, but Dad won't like it."

"He'll never know," Sylvie said, "now will he?"

Jules shook her head. Their dad – and his rules – had left for work almost an hour ago, so he wasn't there to see them. And she wouldn't tell, that was for sure. *We've got each other's backs.*

Both Sylvie and Jules could recite all of Dad's rules by heart:

> *Do not* go out of earshot of the
> house.
> *Do not* mess with wild animals.
> *Do not* miss the bus.
> *Do not*, under any circumstances,
> go near the Slip.

Jules and Sylvie called the rules the "Do Nots". And a snow family by the trail that led to the Slip, even if it was officially still within boundaries, would probably make Dad wonder if they had been on the trail itself. The last and biggest Do Not. Jules reached for her trusty hand lens with its tiny light.

"Come on," said Sylvie. "This snow will all be gone by the time Dad gets home tonight anyway.

There's nothing to worry about. We'll be quick."

That was another difference between them. Sylvie was quick to act and Jules took her time, thought things through. For example, Dad had never said *Do not go out in the snow in your pyjamas,* but Jules was fairly certain that he wouldn't approve, even though they did also have on boots, mittens and hoodies.

Except Sylvie was right. Dad wouldn't know, would he? He was already at work at the lumber mill. It was new, this arrangement where Dad backed the old Dodge Ram pick-up truck down their dirt driveway before the two of them got on the school bus. Jules knew that he didn't like leaving them alone like that, but Sylvie spoke for both of them when she assured him, "We can do it, Dad." And for the past three months it had worked out just fine.

Better than fine, actually. Without Dad hovering over them to keep them in line, they could do things like run out into the new snow and make snow families. Good packing snow was the best kind, and you had to take advantage of it before it got so cold that the snowflakes wouldn't stick together, or too warm so that they melted.

Don't be late for the bus, was another thing Dad said over and over. Then he followed with, *This is Sylvie and Jules's dad, counting on them.*

It was his way of making extra sure that they were paying attention. Jules was pretty certain he wasn't counting on them to make snow families in their PJs, especially when it was close to bus time. But Sylvie was already rolling one tiny ball and then another, intent on her work.

"You make the snow dad and I'll make the daughters," Jules said now.

Making miniature snow families was something they had started long ago: teensy snow fathers and snow children, little families like theirs grouped around the house. Some of the snow families included friends, like the Porters, who lived across the river from them. According to Sylvie, it had been their mother who'd started the tradition. Tiny snow people, easy for tiny humans to make with only a little help.

"Don't forget a snow mom," said Sylvie, and then she added, "I'll make her."

"No!" said Jules. "*I'll* make her." The anger she'd felt just minutes before crept back under her skin.

Sylvie looked startled by the insistence in Jules's voice. Jules could hear it too, but why should Sylvie always get to make the snow mom? Jules patted a small figure together between her blue mittens while Sylvie watched. Then she placed her down next to the snow dad, which Sylvie had stuck right in the middle of the trail, his little stick arms spread wide as if to hold the snow daughters back.

"There," said Jules. "A perfect snow family.

The last one of the season."

But Sylvie reached out, picked up the snow mom and gently set her down right in the middle of the family circle. Jules almost said something – why did Sylvie have to correct her? – but she didn't. There was something in Sylvie's eyes, something that kept Jules quiet. All these years, and Sylvie still missed their mother so much. Jules missed her too, but she knew it wasn't like Sylvie's missing. Sometimes she wondered just how big that kind of missing could be.

"Mom loved new snow," said Sylvie. "Just like us."

Kapow! Like an exclamation point, a faint gunshot echoed. It was distant, likely from across the river.

The bear.

Dad had told them that a rogue bear had been raiding some of the local farmers' chickens. As if to verify the disturbance, a host of birds spoke up. A dozen pairs of cardinals, a small flock of black-capped chicka-dees, tiny wood finches and a bunch of starlings. They all started squawking, and without warning, snow suddenly shook itself off the tree branches and swirled around. Jules drew in a cold breath. It was time to go in. But she could tell with one look that Sylvie had other ideas, ideas that meant leaving Jules alone again.

"No, Sylvie," said Jules. "NO. The bus…"

But Sylvie just smiled. "Plenty of time," she said. "I'll be quick. I have to start getting in shape for track anyway."

Sylvie was the fastest sprinter in the school, the star of the track team. The second fastest was Liz Redding, and she wasn't even close.

"No. Come on, we have to get dressed. Besides, I'm freezing."

But Sylvie stayed put, right there by the snow family. Right there by the trail that led to the Slip.

"I have an errand," she said, and she patted her pocket.

Oh no. No no no. Jules knew what was in there: a wish rock. A quick image of the striped sock in their bedroom closet, bulging with wish rocks, flashed through her head. Had Sylvie taken one out? She must have. Maybe it was the special one, the striped chunk of gneiss that Jules had slipped in there just yesterday, perfect for throwing into the Slip. If Sylvie got it into her head that it was time to take another wish rock to the Slip, nothing, not even Jules, could stop her.

"No," said Jules again. "We're already cutting it close."

Dad would be mad if they missed the bus. He'd be madder still if he knew about the Slip. Jules and Sylvie had never, not once, missed the bus, but what their dad didn't know was that they had gone to the Slip dozens of times, hundreds of times, too many times to count. It wasn't that far from their house, not far at all, just down the trail through the woods. They knew the trail, they knew the sound of the Whippoorwill River's tumbling water and, mostly, they knew just how close they could get to the river's edge.

Besides, there was the Sylvie Sherman Motto: *If we keep our feet dry, we'll be safe.*

And hadn't they always been safe?

Yes, they had.

Jules looked at her sister, standing there next to the tiny snow mom and snow dad and snow sisters. She was wearing her favourite headband, blue with yellow buttercups. It had been their mother's. Sylvie wore it almost every day. All at once, Jules wanted it. If Jules snatched the headband off Sylvie's head, maybe that would distract her from going to the Slip.

"Hey, it's my turn for the headband," she said, reaching for it. "Gimme."

But Sylvie dodged Jules's grasp and set her boots in the snow in a sprinter's crouch.

"Sylvie, *no.*"

Sylvie looked up and smiled. "Try and stop me."

Jules couldn't, and they both knew it. There

was no catching Sylvie. She ran so fast she had a hard time stopping. Time after time Jules had seen her sister take a long skid before coming to a halt. Other times Sylvie grabbed onto tree branches or the porch rail to slow herself down, as if she had no brakes.

"Please, Sylvie. We'll miss the bus."

"Quit worrying," Sylvie said. "I'll be right back."

But the feeling of *no* came swarming up through Jules's whole body. *No. Don't go.* She grabbed Sylvie's hand to keep her from going. *No no no.* But as soon as she did, Sylvie gave a good, hard tug and the orange mitten slipped right off, making Jules stumble backwards. She caught her balance, then waved the mitten in the air, like a flame against the white snow. *Come back!* But Sylvie was already running, her one bare, mittenless hand inside the pocket of her hoodie.

And once again, Jules was left in Sylvie's wake.

4

It was true that Sylvie had never missed the bus. And she was so fast. She would be right back, and then she would get dressed and they'd run out to the end of the driveway and jump on the bus, and there Sam would be, sitting in their usual seat, and they'd all smush in together like always.

Jules went back into the warm house and put her rocks back where they belonged, on the windowsill and the bookshelves and inside the wooden box. She saved the blue-grey slate for last. There. Done. But something didn't feel right, so she took the chunk of marble that Sylvie had given her and put it in her hoodie pocket. That was better.

Sylvie was probably at the Slip by now.

There were lots of stories about the Slip. According to Sam's dad, who was a forest ranger, it was a freak of geology, the result of a seismic shift, a small earthquake that forced the river's bed to disappear into a large cavern that was hiding there all along, opened up by the shifting earth. A hundred metres downstream it bubbled back up into the open air and formed a quiet pool before it remembered that it was a river and needed to ramble its way southward.

That made sense to Jules.

But there was another story, the Legend of the River Brothers, the one that their neighbour Mrs Harless had told them – and Mrs Harless's family had lived beside the river for generations, so she should know.

According to Mrs Harless, it was "a tale of two brothers, both beautiful, who loved the same girl". Each brother longed for the girl, and finally, in frustration, they told her to choose one or the other for her husband. The girl, in despair, said that she couldn't. She loved them both. So the older brother said, "Let the river decide." It was agreed that whichever one of them swam through the underground cavern and came up in the pool first would win the girl's hand. After all, they had seen turtles and even geese dodge under the swirling water and minutes later pop up in the quiet waters of the pool.

With that, both of the boys stripped off their clothes and grabbed for the other's hand. As they leaped from the river's side, they each called to the other, "Brother!" Right away, the smaller and younger panicked. He tried to swim out of the current, tried to make it back to the tree-lined banks. Terrified, the older and stronger brother swam to follow. But it was too late. They couldn't get out of the water's grip. It sucked them down, swallowed them whole.

A hundred metres away, it spat the older one out, barely alive, his body battered and scratched from the tree roots that stretched below ground like a ropy sieve, trapping limbs and leaves and turtles. His skin was bruised from being knocked against the rocks that jutted into the darkness. He was so weak he could barely pull himself onto the banks.

But the younger brother. Where was he? The older brother called and called and called. But there was no answer. The river kept him as a prize.

When the older brother recovered, he married the girl in a small, sad ceremony that seemed all the smaller for the absence of his brother. What the older brother didn't tell anyone was that something else had happened underneath the earth where the water flowed.

The boy and the girl grew older. They had many children. At last the time came for them to pass on, and the boy-no-longer-beautiful could not contain his terrible secret for another day. Finally he confessed.

"I had his hand. I was trying to pull him up with me, trying and trying. But I wasn't strong enough, and in the end I ... I let go."

And all the tears that the old man had held inside for so many years streamed down his cheeks.

The story of the River Brothers had always made Jules worry. The thought of the Slip, being sucked underground by the force of the water, made her heart race. And that was just fine with their dad.

Don't ever *go near the Slip.*

How many times had he told them that? So many. Despite his rigid rules, Jules loved her quiet, strong dad. Chess Sherman. She loved the way he hummed while he read the newspaper and how, after he checked their homework at night, he said, "This is Sylvie and Jules's dad, signing off."

Jules knew that whenever he started a sentence with "This is Jules and Sylvie's dad", it was almost the same as a hug. He had never been big on telling them that he loved them, but Jules knew that he did by the way he said that sentence, like he was so very glad that he was Jules and Sylvie's dad, their dad, their sweet dad. And somehow, knowing that he claimed them like that helped take up the space that their mother had left. For her, anyway, if not for Sylvie. For Dad was living and breathing and right there with them, to remind them of the Do Nots and to sign off on their homework and to make sure they ate their dinners and did their chores. To count on them and to take care of them.

But Jules's memory of their mother was disappearing, just like their mom's favourite mug, the one with the flamingo on it, had disappeared without a trace. It had sat on the windowsill above the kitchen sink for as long as Jules could remember, and then one day it wasn't there. Frantic, Jules had searched all over the house for it. Sylvie too. But it was gone.

Gone, like their mother.

"Maybe Dad moved it," Sylvie had said. "Maybe it made him too sad."

Jules didn't want her dad to be sad. So she never brought up the missing mug, even when she saw Dad standing at the empty windowsill with his head tilted as if he, too, was confused.

Mostly what Jules remembered about her mother was the mustard jar, and how it had fallen from the bag of groceries that her mother had been carrying and burst open at the foot of the porch steps, scattering pieces of yellow-smeared glass on the gravelly walk, and how her mother had said, "Oh!" in surprise just before she crumpled, her body folded in on itself.

Jules had watched Sylvie tug and tug on their mother's still shoulder, then watched some more as her sister took off running on the frozen path between their house and Mrs Harless's back door, running to fetch Mrs Harless, while Jules stood there, unable to move. She couldn't even look at her crumpled-in-half mother at all, only at the bits of yellow glass, like brilliant chips from the sun itself.

"Hurry, hurry, hurry!" Jules had screamed to Sylvie.

And Sylvie had hurried. She had run as fast as a deer, as fast as a lynx, as fast as a six-year-old girl could run. But no matter how fast Sylvie ran, Mrs Harless couldn't save their mother. No one could.

Later Mrs Harless pulled them both onto the sofa and sang to them, sang so softly that only they could hear it, sang so that at last both of them stopped sobbing.

Heart defect, was what they said — doctor, ambulance driver. Dad.

Then: Six years ago. A broken jar of mustard.

Now: A missing flamingo mug.

She loved you girls, her father told them, over and over.

Not too long after their mother died, Sylvie told Jules that sometimes she felt as if their mom was watching them, like she wasn't that far away.

"Like where would she be?" said Jules. "On the roof, maybe?"

Sylvie didn't think so. It was then that they made up the Maybe game. It always started with the same question:

What happens after you die?

Then they took turns answering:

Maybe you turn into wind.

Maybe you turn into stars.

Maybe you go to another world.

Now Jules sat down on her bed. She rubbed her finger along the chunk of marble. She wished she knew for sure that their mom was still watching them. *Maybe.* Then she jumped up. She didn't want to think about the Maybe game unless Sylvie was there to play it with her. So she pulled on her jeans and her shirt and her sweatshirt over that, tugged on the lanyard that held her hand lens and then waited for her sister to get back. Sylvie was cutting it close, but there was still time.

Any minute now.

5

On the other side of the river from the Shermans' woods, Sam Porter pulled his woolly hat over his ears and set off down the long drive toward the road where he would catch the school bus. His two best friends, Sylvie and Jules Sherman, used to call him Super Friend Sam. Once in a while Jules still did. He didn't mind, even though he was in seventh grade. Not when it came from Jules. Besides, she never called him that outside the woods.

Kapow! The distant sound of a rifle made him stop in his tracks. It wasn't wild turkey season yet, and deer season was long over. Maybe someone was trying to scare off a coyote? Or that bear that had supposedly been roaming around? He had heard his dad talk about a yearling bear that had been spotted near Archer's Sheep Farm, and Mr Archer was determined to get rid of it. Sam wondered what the bear was doing out. Even though it was late March, it still seemed early for a bear to be done with hibernation.

He listened hard. There was nothing, only the distant rush of the Whippoorwill. Maybe, he thought, the snow would force the bear back into its den. He hoped so, for the sake of both the bear and the sheep.

Sam fastened the top button of his thick coat, then stuffed his hands deep into his pockets, feeling for the rock in his right pocket. It was about the size of the medal his older brother, Elk, had been awarded in Afghanistan. It was a wish rock, one that Jules had found for him by the river, Jules with her special pick hammer and her hand lens. It was a rock that he would return to the river as soon as he could, his burning wish written on it in waterproof marker.

He looked down. The new wet snow covered the leather toes of his boots. It was just the kind of snow that Sylvie and Jules loved. They were probably out in front of their house right now, hurrying to make one of their snow families before the bus came. Sam loved those snow families, especially when one included a miniature Sam. He headed towards the road to wait for the school bus. The walk wasn't far, not even half a mile, but he had left his house early so that he could take his time. Today he was on the lookout for something. Something special.

"You never know," he said out loud to a small grey squirrel that chattered at him from the branches of the towering maple tree next to the drive. The squirrel did not reply, just shook its tail and darted away.

An enormous snowflake fell right on his nose. He rubbed it off. It wasn't unusual for late March to bring a fresh snow. This was Vermont after all. In Sam's eleven and a half years, he had seen snow fall every month except July and August – and who knows, if he lived there long enough, he might see it then, too.

But on that morning there was the possibility of seeing something else he had never seen. He had woken up to reports of it on the radio – a sighting of a fabled animal just to the north of the Whippoorwill.

Catamount. Sam even loved the name of him, like he was part cat, part mountain.

He wasn't the same as a bobcat or a lynx. No, the catamount was in the same family as the pumas of Florida and the western mountain lions of California and North Dakota. He was kin to the painters of Kentucky and Tennessee. They all had the same large square face and long, swooping tail. They all shared a singular secretiveness. Nevertheless, Sam knew that the catamount was its own distinct cat – an eastern cougar. And while none had been definitively spotted since the 1930s, every year someone reported a sighting. Just thinking about it, Sam's pulse quickened. The thought of the catamount was why he had left home early.

"Every year there's a sighting," his dad had told him, "but a sighting isn't the same as a real catamount." His dad was a forest ranger. Sam knew he was right, but still. It meant a possibility. A sighting meant *maybe*.

"Probably just a lynx or a bobcat," his mom had added. "One of those would be more likely. No catamounts around here in dozens of years."

But that didn't mean there wasn't one here now.

"Catamount," Sam whispered. He wrapped

his hand around the rock, felt the wish burning there in his palm. He had faith in wish rocks. And Jules found him the best ones. For a whole year he had wished for his older brother, Elk, to come home from Afghanistan. He had wished it over and over on an entire year's worth of rocks. *Elk return.* And hadn't that wish come true? Only a few weeks ago, his brother had returned.

Sam started walking again, faster this time. He couldn't wait to tell Jules and Sylvie about the catamount sighting. Every morning and afternoon, even though the bus seats were only designed for two, the three of them smushed together on one seat, Sam right in the middle.

Growing up, hardly a day had passed without Sylvie and Jules and Sam together.

Jules: Eleven.

Sam: Eleven and a half.

Sylvie: Twelve.

They knew the wooded acres of their properties inside out. Their neighbour Mrs Harless even called them "woodland creatures". Sam rubbed the rock between his fingers.

Catamount return.

He would take it to the Slip and throw it into the rushing water, the way he and Jules and Sylvie had done for years. It was against the rules, of course. The Porter rules were no different from the Sherman rules. *Do not, under any circumstances, go to the Slip.*

Sam didn't go out of his way to break rules, but when it came to wish rocks, the Slip rule was one that he chose to ignore. And now his brother, Elk, was home safe and sound. Wasn't it possible that the wish rocks might have had *something* to do with that? And now ... a catamount. One wish had come true and now maybe another was about to.

Then again, there was Mrs Harless's wish, the

one that did not come true: *Zeke return.* Zeke Harless, her grandson, the boy she'd raised ever since his parents died in a car accident. Zeke who was Elk's best friend. Zeke who had gone with Elk to Afghanistan. Sam knew that Mrs Harless had thrown dozens of wish rocks into the Slip too, all with that same message.

And in the days since he had been back, Elk hadn't said anything about Zeke. In fact he had said only a few words, period. Elk had given his medal to their dad, and when their dad tried to give it back to him he just shook his head. Each day he slipped out of the house and faded into the woods.

"Leave him be," their dad told Sam.

Sam had tried to leave him be, but it was hard. Elk was home after being gone for a whole entire year, but it didn't feel the same. It was as if a different version of his brother had come back from the war.

"We have to be patient," his mom told him. "Your brother came back, but Zeke didn't. Elk needs time. He has to figure out how to get along now."

Would things ever get back to normal? That was Sam's question, but he didn't ask it. His mom and dad were worried enough as it was. It was good to have school to go to, and Sylvie and Jules to roam the woods with. And a wish rock in his pocket.

Sam picked up his pace. Snow. New snow.

Then the morning cracked open with the sharp cry of a fox, and Sam smiled. Everyone knew that a fox meant luck.

6

Jules kicked the new snow with the toe of her boot. She rolled Sylvie's mitten into an orange ball between her own blue mittens and held it under her nose. It smelled warm, like Sylvie. What was taking her so long? The Slip was close. How long did it take to chuck one single wish rock into it? They were going to miss the bus!

When Mrs Harless had told them the story about the River Brothers, she'd also told them about the wish rocks. She said that if a wish was good enough it would glimmer in the deep, dark shadows below the water, and pretty soon it would become so bright it would turn into an underwater star. And if that happened, there was a good chance that the wish would be granted.

"But it has to be something you want more than anything else in the whole world," said Mrs Harless. "It has to be a burning wish."

Of course, thought Jules. Didn't rocks come from stars anyway? Some of them did. And didn't they also burn as they fell through the sky?

Together, she and Sylvie and Sam had tossed hundreds, maybe thousands, of wish rocks into the Slip. They used a waterproof marker so that their wishes wouldn't ever wash off.

The only trouble was, Jules didn't have a burning wish. Only small, daily wishes, like *no washing dishes* or *a silver dollar from the tooth fairy* or *watermelon for dinner.* Well, her Estwing E13P hammer had been a pretty big wish, but it still seemed small compared to Sam's and Sylvie's wishes. Their wishes were huge.

From for ever, Jules had known that Sam's burning wish was for the catamount to return. But when Zeke and Elk went to Afghanistan, Sam's wish changed. *Elk return*. And Elk did return, which meant that Sam's burning wish had probably gone back to *Catamount return*.

Before he left for Afghanistan, Elk had come by and taken Jules aside.

"Listen, Jules," he had said. "I'm going to ask you to do something for me."

He had put both hands on her shoulders and looked right into her eyes. Elk was usually quiet and serious, but when he laughed, everyone else around him laughed too, especially his best friend, Zeke. They used to set each other off. But there had been no laughter about him just then. It was only her and Elk, on the porch of Jules's house.

"Sam's going to be throwing wish rocks into

the river for me until I get back," Elk said.

Jules nodded. Of course he was. She waited while Elk shifted from one foot to the other. Finally he said, "If we don't come home, would you take these to the Grotto?"

He reached for her hand and placed two agates into it. Agate was one of her favourite rocks. She brought them up close to her eyes and studied them. They were nearly identical, in size and shape and colour and markings. Had she ever seen two rocks so closely matched?

Then Elk took a breath and let it out slowly. "To honour Zeke and me?" he said.

He pressed her fingers around the agates. For a second Jules didn't understand what he was asking, then she did.

"Can you do that?" He looked directly at her, then tapped her fingers, curled around the twin agates. Jules wasn't sure what to say. She was proud that Elk had trusted her with them. But she had no idea where to find the Grotto, or even if it really existed.

So far as Jules knew, it was just a myth, a cave of sorts, rumoured to be somewhere in the woods of the Sherman tract. It had been there for centuries, hidden. "Some think it might have been used by the Abenaki," Mrs Harless had told them. "Others think the Norsemen ... the Vikings ... thought of it as a sacred space. It wouldn't surprise me."

Legend had it that the cave was filled with rocks: rare rocks and ordinary rocks, rocks collected and brought there from all over New England and even beyond, from Iceland and the Arctic Circle and Russia.

"A kind of memorial," Mrs Harless had added. "Whether to the living or the dead, no one knows. There's supposed to be a significance to every single rock in it. Even if we don't know what that significance is."

That made sense to Jules. Every single rock in her own collection was significant, each for a different reason. But how could she make a promise when she didn't know how to find a place that maybe wasn't real?

"Rock Girl," Elk had said. "If anyone can find the Grotto, it'll be you. That's why you're the one I'm asking." Then he smiled, one of his rare grins. And Jules couldn't help it. She smiled back at him.

"So I have your solemn word?"

"You have my solemn word," Jules promised.

But it was a promise that Jules hadn't kept. She still had the twin agates, so similar to each other that they looked practically identical. She knew that she should return them to Elk, but she hadn't. And Zeke?

Mrs Harless's burning wish that her grandson would come home safe had not come true.

As for Sylvie? Sylvie had only one wish, and it burned so hard that Jules was sometimes afraid to touch her sister's wish rocks, afraid they would scorch her from the force of that one wish, which was always the same: *Run faster*. Sometimes she would add *faster than a deer*. Sometimes she would write *faster than a comet*. And sometimes: *faster than a rocket*.

But why? Why did Sylvie want to go so fast? Jules had asked her a million times.

Jules: "Why?"

Sylvie: "So that..." she would begin, as if she

was thinking of the best way to answer Jules. But she never did. Jules would wait and wait, but that was all Sylvie said, that first time and every time thereafter. *So that.*

The lack of an answer did not keep Jules from asking, and sometimes Sylvie would say something like "So that ... I can break the sound barrier", or "So that ... I can leave a vapour trail behind me", or "So that ... I can win the Kentucky Derby". Jules knew that none of those answers were true, and Sylvie knew she knew.

So what was the truth? Jules didn't know and Sylvie wouldn't say.

Now Jules stood on the porch looking at the trail to the Slip. Less than fifteen minutes ago, Sylvie had leaped right over the new little snow family, right over the miniature snow dad's stick arms spread wide to stop her. She should be leaping back any second now.

The woods felt hugely quiet. Too quiet.

Then, in the very thick of the silence, Jules heard the quick, high-pitched cry of a fox. She recognized it immediately. There was no other sound like it: a "vixen's cry" was what Mrs Harless called it.

A fox! Foxes meant luck.

Jules jumped back off the porch and over to the little snow family. She took her mittens off, and with her bare hands – yikes, cold! – patted together a miniature snow fox and set it next to the arms-out snow dad. She admired it, the bushy little tail, the alert tilt to its head. Sylvie would like it too.

"Sylvie!" Jules shouted to the empty trail. The Slip wasn't *that* far. Jules crouched next to the new little snow fox and trained her eyes down the path, willing her sister to appear. The groan and wheeze of the school bus came to her ears. Then there it was, at the bottom of the driveway. Oh no.

"SYLVIE!" she yelled again. "COME ON!"

They were going to miss the bus for the first time ever, and not because of Jules. How would they explain this to Dad? The anger she had felt earlier returned full force. Enough of this.

She took off down the trail, jumping right over the new snow family, the tiny snow fox next to the tiny worried snow dad. She ran right next to Sylvie's tracks, which were clear and fresh in the brand-new snow.

"Sylvie!" Jules cried again.

But there was no answer. There were only Sylvie's empty tracks, quickly filling up with wet snow. Now Jules could hear the river. The sound of it grew louder. She was almost there. She would see her sister any second now. Sylvie would be standing by the river. *If we keep our feet dry, we'll be safe.* That's what she always said. It was the Sylvie Sherman Motto. Sylvie Sherman was about to get an earful from her sister.

And then, suddenly ... a tree root, barely jutting up in the new snow. And just beyond, Sylvie's tracks became a wide gash, a gash that shot straight into the Whippoorwill. Water rushed in front of Jules and disappeared into the Slip. The roar of it filled her ears.

"SYLVIE!"

Jules turned in a circle, stumbled in her wet boots. She screamed her sister's name. And screamed it again. The air above the water was empty, a hole that Sylvie had fallen through.

Jules turned away from the awful emptiness and looked back down the path. Boot prints. Her own and Sylvie's, side by side. She looked towards Mrs Harless's place. Nothing. Only new snow. She looked across the river at the Porters'. Nothing. She forced herself to look down again. The barely jutting-up root, the gash. Water streamed into the opening of the Slip, rushing over the ancient stones, stones that looked like jagged teeth.

Jules's knees buckled. She gulped in the frozen air. But she knew: there was not enough air in the whole entire world that could make the river give Sylvie back.

PART TWO

8

The mother fox pressed herself as hard as she could into the leaves.

Three kits were growing inside her, a girl and two boys. She could already sense the personalities of the brothers. One was agile and focused, the other calm and strong.

But the third, the female, she was a mystery. Her physical body was forming itself — was nearly formed now — but her spirit still lingered somewhere else. Aloof. That her daughter's spirit was so late in arriving made the mother fox anxious. Why had it not happened yet?

The babies pushed against her rib cage and she licked her belly, as if to reassure them. She wished again that her little girl's spirit would hurry.

Then she startled. Something, unexpected and unplanned, was happening to a creature near by. She crouched low, scenting the air. Whatever was happening was chaotic and full of fear. The fact that it was happening to another creature, that she and her unborn kits were safe tucked into the underbrush, didn't help her unease.

The two brother kits inside her squirmed and pushed, nearly full term and ready to be born.

And the girl?

The mother fox focused on the blood and bones and beating heart of the mysterious female kit inside her. She tried to ignore the confusion and panic floating all around her in the freezing air.

Then a sudden, weary peace rushed through her.

Her daughter's spirit had arrived. The mother fox sensed it, swift and nimble, finding its way to the little body waiting within. But as she sighed, she felt a deep, deep stirring. A thousand years of fox knowledge washed over her, knowledge of the hunt, knowledge of the seasons, and something else. In her ancient memory she heard the ancestors whisper, *Kennen*.

Kennen.

There are, in the animal world, those who are known as totems. They serve as bearers of luck and good fortune. People carve their likenesses into teak and bone and serpentine, then carry them in their pockets or wear them on chains around their necks.

There are stories also of familiars, creatures who serve their masters in matters of magic and spells. Witches, we're told, are particularly fond of cats and frogs.

And then there are the rarest of all, the Kennen.

73

It's said that before any creature is born, it is linked to something. Some are linked to trees, some are linked to sky. Still others are linked to rain or wind or stars. But the Kennen? They are linked to the spirits. No one is sure why. Some believe that the Kennen are meant to finish something that isn't finished, to settle something that needs to be settled. Others say that a Kennen's true purpose is to help in some way, big or small. It's hard to tell, so rare are they.

What is known is that the Kennen come to this world for reasons beyond our knowing, and once their missions are done, they return to the haven of their ancestors. In an instant, the mother fox understood that her daughter would not belong wholly to her or these Vermont woods. She also knew that it didn't matter. She would love her little girl fox as hard as any mother could, maybe harder.

But for now, her kits safe inside her, she lifted

her face towards the sky and cried into the morning air, a greeting to the day and the new knowledge that the falling snow had brought with it.

9

The sheriff and the bloodhounds stood for hours and hours beside the Whippoorwill, at the place where the water re-emerged from its underground path, to see if Sylvie's body would float up on the tumbling currents.

The sheriff even requested additional help further downstream in case his crew had missed her. Finally they all gathered in the Sherman kitchen, and Jules heard them tell how they'd dragged a net across the river, but all they'd snagged were tree limbs and a piece of rusted metal that looked like it had been in the water for decades. They had all traipsed back and forth from the house to the river so many times that the new snow family had been obliterated. There was no sign of them, not even the little snow fox.

The sheriff sat down at their kitchen table. "There's nothing, Chess," he said. There was not a single article of her clothing, either. No boots. No headband. No single orange mitten. No pyjamas. Nothing.

"We'll keep looking," Jules heard the sheriff say.

A small bead of hope filled Jules's chest. They'd dragged the river. They hadn't found anything. They *hadn't*. As long as they hadn't found Sylvie in the river, she could still be alive, couldn't she?

But where? And what about the hounds? Wouldn't they be able to track her? As if in answer, the sheriff said, "Hard to track on snow, especially after it's melted." He paused,

then added, "We did flush out a young bear. Sidetracked the hounds for a bit. Looked like it might be injured. Or just dumb, sticking too close to humans."

A bear, thought Jules. Maybe Sylvie had been attacked by a bear? But the hounds ... the small bead of hope rolled away. She knew in her heart there was only one place that Sylvie could be. Jules had seen the root sticking up in the path, she'd seen the gash in the snow that led past the stone teeth. The men knew it too; she had led them there.

Yes, she nodded. Yes. She had even told Dad about Sylvie's wishes. *Run faster,* every rock said. Every single one. Always. *Faster than an osprey. Faster than light. Faster than a cheetah.* Jules had told them everything.

His shoulders started shaking, and he covered his face with his hands. A sob worked its way up into Jules's throat. Dad rubbed his eyes, pulled her close and wrapped his arms around her. He rubbed her back, right between her shoulder blades. Just like she always imagined her mother might have done when she was a baby. The sob escaped her in a huge flood of tears. "Dad," she gasped.

"It's OK, Juley-Jules," he whispered. "It's OK." And right there, in front of the sheriff, he said, "My little girl," and even though she wasn't little any more, not at all, she climbed up into his lap like she had a long time ago, and he rocked her, back and forth, back and forth, like he had when she was so much younger.

"Juley-Jules," he said again, his pet name for her. "It's OK." She held on as hard as she could.

But it wasn't OK.

Sylvie was gone.

And Sylvie being gone was the worst "not OK" in the universe. Jules had not tried hard enough. If she had yelled and screamed at Sylvie to stay there, maybe Sylvie wouldn't have gone to the Slip. If she hadn't put that chunk of gneiss in the striped sock in the closet, knowing that Sylvie would think it was a perfect wish rock, then maybe Sylvie wouldn't have gone to the Slip. If she had grabbed better hold of Sylvie, her hand and not just her mitten, then maybe she could've kept her there. She hadn't held on tight enough. There was the single orange mitten, right there on the table. Proof.

At last Dad stopped rocking and handed her a tea towel to wipe her stinging face.

"I love you," he whispered.

And Jules knew that was a true thing, so true it made her heart hurt even more because he loved Sylvie just as much. Maybe even more. And she and Sylvie had broken the biggest Do Not. How many times had their dad told them never to go near the Slip? So many.

"It's my fault, Dad," she sobbed, pushing the

tea towel away. "I should have made her stay."

She felt him shake his head against her own. "No," he said. "You and I both know that nobody can make Sylvie do anything."

That might be true, but it only made it worse. Jules felt an alarming flash of anger at her sister. If only Sylvie hadn't run so fast. If only she had stopped in time. If only the tree root hadn't been there. If only the snow hadn't covered it up. Sylvie would have seen it. She would have kept her feet dry if only, if only, if only. If Sylvie were there this very minute, Jules would scream at her the way she'd wanted to this morning, when she'd shut herself into their bedroom.

But Sylvie wasn't there. Sylvie wasn't ever going to be there again.

That was the worst thought of all, so horrible that Jules's mind scrabbled for a way out of it. Now she snatched the tea towel back to stanch the flood of tears that wouldn't stop pouring from her eyes. Dad held her tighter.

The Maybe game came into her head.

Maybe you turn into an albatross and fly across the ocean.

Maybe you turn into a giant sea turtle and crawl up on the sand by the light of the moon.

Maybe you turn into a mermaid and swim around the world.

She wiped her face again. The game wasn't helping. She couldn't see Sylvie as a bird or a turtle or even a mermaid. She could only see her as Sylvie, running and running and running, her hair swinging back and forth across her shoulders, the blue hair band with buttercups pushed behind her ears. Running so fast. *So that* … what? Why was Sylvie's burning wish to run faster?

How would Jules ever find out now?

10

The baby girl fox, Senna, came into the world in darkness, ten metres below ground in the den dug out of cool brown earth. She was the middle child, born between her older and younger brothers, the three of them separated by minutes.

The first thing she knew was the feel of her mother's tongue. *Shhh shhh shhh,* cleaning her off, licking her into life and warmth and love and safety.

The second thing she knew was the feel and smell of her brothers' bodies pressed against hers as their mother nursed them, their front paws kneading her belly.

The third thing she knew was that there was someone waiting for her, someone she needed to find. After the rough tongue of her mother had given her a second cleaning and smoothed her wet fur, Senna sniffed in the darkness. Back and forth she rolled, pressing her paws into her sleeping brothers' backs and bellies. Despite her mother's warm milk, she didn't go to sleep like her brothers.

Sleep, said her mother in the language of fox. *Sleep, little Senna.*

Baby Senna lay awake and quiet. She wriggled her way closer into the soft fur of her mother's hide. She sniffed the air and smelled her sleeping brothers, her sleeping father. *Sleep,* her mother told her again, *sleep, little girl.*

Where was the Someone?

She cocked her tiny round ears and listened,

but there were only the sleeping sounds of her brothers and father, only the rough tongue of her mother. Finally Senna closed her eyes and drifted off. But as she did, a whispery word flowed over her from somewhere far away. *Kennen.* The word appeared to her as bars of grey and forest green hanging in the air, drifting towards one another, passing through one another, always moving.

Kennen, the bars whispered. Senna watched in the darkness of the den, and as she did, the grey-green bars passed on through her, leaving behind small bits of worry and wonder, like invisible drops on her newborn fur.

11

Every day that Elk had been at war, Sam had written a wish on a rock, *Elk return*. And Elk had come back. But Sam knew that his brother wasn't completely home. It was as if Afghanistan had kept a part of Elk and sent the rest of him back to his family.

Elk Porter and Zeke Harless had been best friends their whole lives. They had enlisted in the army together and they had been deployed to Afghanistan together. The Shermans, the Porters, Mrs Harless, all of them had gone to the airport to wave goodbye. They had stood under the steel-blue sky as the aeroplane lifted Elk and Zeke off and carried them thousands of miles away to the other side of the world.

If Sam had known that it would be the last time he'd see Zeke, would he have said something to him besides "Bye, Zeke"? Would he have done anything differently while Zeke and Elk were gone? Should he have thrown wish rocks for Zeke, too? Would that have made any difference?

It was impossible to know.

Before they shipped out, Sam had hardly known a day without his brother or Zeke. Now Elk was home and Zeke was not, and Elk hadn't said a single word about Zeke. If anyone mentioned him, Elk stood up and walked out of the room.

Now Sam sat on the empty seat of the school bus, heading home. He pressed his forehead against the cold glass window and looked out into the passing trees. Tall and solemn, they looked weary from the long winter that never seemed to end.

They were passing the border of Mrs Harless's property. It was said that her great-great-great-grandfather had marked his tract with rock cairns. No one knew specifically where the originals were now. Some of them had likely been knocked apart by growing trees, or pulled over by bears searching for grubs. Some might have been toppled by the Whippoorwill when she flowed out of her banks after a heavy thaw.

Elk and Zeke used to hunt for cairns all the time. They'd found five or six, and when Sam was big enough they let him tag along too. But there was something else made of rock that they all wanted to find: the Grotto, which wasn't a true cairn so much as a shallow cave. It was thought that the rocks surrounding the entrance might be carefully placed in an orderly way, like those stacked in an old gate, maybe, or an old archway. They had looked for it all one summer, along with Sylvie and Jules, searching along the animal trails and along the paths that led to the Slip on both the Sherman and Porter sides of the river, looking for anything that might be a rock structure or a cave entrance.

All they'd found were a bunch of stone walls and the foundation of an old cabin. But abandoned foundations and crumbling stone walls were everywhere in Vermont, bordering roads and property, marking trailheads and rights of way. They'd even found some of the old original cairns, or what might have once been old cairns: a stack of rocks that seemed too even for nature to have set it that way, or a set of matched stones that were criss-crossed in a certain manner.

But no Grotto. And that was what they truly wanted to find. Especially Jules, with her fascination for rocks. Jules, with her special hammer and her hand lens that she wore on a lanyard around her neck. Half the time Jules's backpack was weighed down more with rocks than books. Elk even called her Rock Girl.

As Sam stared out the bus window, the trees looked as lonely as he felt. Elk was probably out there right now, driving his four-wheeler along the old paths, stirring up the birds.

Was it possible, somehow, that Zeke's spirit was out there in the woods? What about Sylvie's spirit?

Just as Elk couldn't talk about Zeke, Sam had a hard time thinking about Sylvie. It had been weeks since she drowned. Two, maybe even three. Sam hadn't tried to keep track. All he knew was that they hadn't found her. His throat tightened, and he pulled his jacket up around his ears. And as he did, a flash of rusty red flickered between the trees. He sat back. Blinked.

"Fox," he said, turning automatically to tell Sylvie and Jules. But of course neither of them were there. And the fox he'd heard the day Sylvie drowned hadn't brought anyone any luck, had it?

He stared at his knees, willing himself not to cry. All he wanted was to get home. One stop. Another. Finally it was his turn. As the driver pulled up to the end of his family's driveway, he hurried down the aisle, not looking at anyone as the bus rolled to a stop.

He tore down the steps, ready to run up the driveway, but someone stood in his way.

Elk. The bus lumbered away as Elk hauled Sam into his arms and squeezed him hard. So hard it felt good.

12

In the above world, the days grew longer. In the birthing den, Senna and her brothers grew too. Fast, the way little foxes do. Soon their parents would lead them through the complicated earthen tunnels to stand at the brink of the above world.

In the meantime, there were the brothers. Older Brother smelled of milk and earth, Younger Brother of fur and pine sap. Older Brother was the quiet, calm one. Except when Senna began batting him with her paw.

Play with me! Play!

And up he leaped, paws out.

Pounce!

Growling and pushing, *bat bat bat*. Older Brother and Senna rolled and wrestled and nipped gently, gently.

Senna. Older Brother. They hated being apart more than even a few centimetres, down there in the below-world den.

Younger Brother, on the other hand, had their father's restless nature. He couldn't wait for the above world. He wanted to trot through the woods, along the trails. He wanted to hunt.

Senna knew about the above world. She did not know how she did, but there it was. She also knew that Older Brother would welcome the sun and the wind. He would be happy. He appeared in Senna's mind as a brown ceramic jug on a flat rock by the river. Younger Brother would be trotting off, muzzle to the air; he appeared to her as a shiny piece of twisted tin, flashing sparks in the sun.

What would Senna herself be like? Her paws itched to be out there, running. She could feel the dry earth underneath her pads, smell the clear, sunny air of day and the starry sky of night.

It wouldn't be long now. Senna could hardly wait. The grey-green bars hovered in the air of the den, colliding into one another, whispering.

And while the mother fox watched her babies grow she knew that soon, very soon, she would need to lead them to the above world.

But not yet. She wasn't ready yet.

13

Jules now lived in a new time called After Sylvie.

After Sylvie, Dad drew a line between their yard and the woods. It was the newest Do Not. He had taken Jules's hand as if she were a toddler and walked her in a circle around the perimeter of their unfenced yard. "*Do not* leave this area," he said. Even though the line was unseeable, Jules knew it was there. "Not to be crossed," her father said. On the other side of it was the rest of the world: the woods, the river, the fields, the road, the bridge, Sam's house across the river. The Slip was there too.

After Sylvie, all Jules could think about was the Slip.

After Sylvie, Mrs Harless came by their house every day and brought them soup. Split pea soup. Cabbage soup. Chicken soup with noodles. Soup that never seemed to cool down.

After Sylvie, the bus quit stopping at the end of their drive because Jules stopped going to school. She couldn't stand the thought of it. Getting on the school bus without Sylvie, walking through the big double doors without Sylvie, facing all her friends, all Sylvie's friends, everyone either looking at her or trying not to look at her.

No.

After Sylvie, Dad stayed home from work. He couldn't bear to leave Jules even for a minute. Jules didn't mind. She didn't want to be alone without her sister.

After Sylvie, Jules organized and reorganized

her rock collection every day. She spread them out on her bed like always. Then she rearranged them into dozens of Sherman Galaxies, beaming the tiny LED sun across their glistening surfaces, shining her magnifier on them so that she could see the nearly invisible lines and cracks, the small chips of mica or pyrite or talc. But she ignored the categories – metamorphic, igneous, sedimentary. She still knew their names, but she didn't want to separate them. No more perfect vertical and horizontal rows. Just the far-flung Sherman Galaxies.

"Do you want to look through your rocks out in the kitchen?" her dad had said to her a couple of times. "Or the living room?"

Jules shook her head. When she was in the bedroom she was forced to look at Sylvie's bed and Sylvie's things and Sylvie's clothes – but that was one thing she didn't mind. In fact, she liked being in their bedroom. Sometimes she talked to

Sylvie, low enough so that her dad couldn't hear her. Why shouldn't she?

After Sylvie, Jules also talked to her rocks. Again, why shouldn't she? None of them ever turned away from her. None of them disappeared. None of them left her standing alone with an orange mitten in her hand. When she set a rock in a particular spot in the galaxy orbit, it stayed there. It never moved except when she moved it.

After Sylvie, she shoved the striped sock, with its dozen or so wish rocks, as far back in the closet as she could, then covered it up with an old beach towel from the stack at the top of the linen pantry. The wish rocks. If she had never found those wish rocks ... perfectly smooth rocks, perfect for throwing across the water, for throwing into the Slip, for carrying a burning wish into the Whippoorwill River on its way to the sea. If Jules could bring herself to dump out the rocks from the striped sock, she would take her hammer, the Estwing E13P, and smash those perfect rocks to smithereens. It wouldn't matter that her hammer wasn't made for smashing. It would do the job. She hated those rocks.

After Sylvie, Jules put the twin agates that Elk had given her underneath Sylvie's pillow until she could give them back to Elk. She *should* give them back to Elk, but she couldn't. Not yet. And Elk had not asked for them anyway.

After Sylvie, Dad laced and then untied, then relaced his boots, and then sat there staring at them as if he didn't know whether to relace them once more.

After Sylvie, Jules caught Dad more than once pouring two glasses of milk, then pouring the second one back into the carton. Her dad didn't drink milk.

After Sylvie, Jules poured the rest of Sylvie's coconut shampoo down the drain of the shower. Even though there was no trace of the shampoo,

Sylvie's signature scent lingered in the bathroom, clung to the shower curtain, hung there in the steamy air. Jules used her dad's Old Spice shampoo when she took a shower. It didn't smell like coconut.

After Sylvie, Jules stood in the kitchen and watched Dad stir a pot of spaghetti sauce. It was the first time since— It was the first time they were eating something beside Mrs Harless's soups. She was sick of Mrs Harless's soup, even though she knew that Mrs Harless was just trying to be nice to them.

The sauce bubbled, thick and spicy. Jules made a salad and her dad dished up the spaghetti and they sat down and ate it at the table where Jules had set down three plates before she remembered.

Again.

Every day she forgot and then every day she remembered.

And that's how it was After Sylvie.

Forget.

Remember.

Forget.

Remember.

Forget.

Remember.

Remember.

Remember.

After Sylvie.

14

Midmorning. The spring days were getting warmer. Jules slumped on the bottom step of the porch and leaned against her father. She looked at the invisible line. "Dad," she started to say, but he interrupted.

"Not to be crossed," he reminded her. For a second she felt a jolt of anger. She didn't need to be reminded about crossing the line, did she? She, after all, wasn't the one who had run down the trail to the Slip. But just as quickly as that thought popped into her head, another one did: why? Why did Sylvie have to go so fast?

For the millionth time, *why*?

The anger sat on her shoulders like a nasty sunburn.

Then, "Jules, you're going to have to go back," her dad told her. "We both have to go back. Next week."

His voice was low and sad. Jules knew he was right, but she couldn't think about it yet. Kids had to go to school and grown-ups had to go to work. That was the way it was. She knew the thought of it was horrible for her dad – she could tell by the way he could barely bring himself to go to the store for groceries.

"Dad," she started to say again, but—

"No, Jules. You're going back next week, and so am I. It's settled."

"That wasn't what I was going to say!"

He looked at her, waiting for her to speak. But what was she going to say? She had no idea. She opened her mouth to try to get a few words to come out: any words. Nothing.

And then her dad got up and walked back into the house. "I'm going to go inside and take a long, hot shower," he told her. Then he left her there, on the porch steps, her mouth full of unspoken words. *Sylvie would've known what to say to him,* thought Jules, and then she felt furious with herself for being jealous of her sister, who wasn't there to fight with, who wasn't... She shook the thought away.

And right then, perched on the bottom step of the porch, the invisible line glowing in the morning sun, her anger spiked again, and this time her mouth cooperated. She spoke directly to Sylvie.

"I'm wearing your Flo-Jo shirt. And you can't stop me, either, so ha ha."

If Sylvie were alive, Jules wouldn't have spoken to her in that way. Not that Jules would be wearing Sylvie's precious Flo-Jo shirt if she were alive.

Nope. That wouldn't be happening. The thought of Sylvie's outrage made Jules almost smile.

"Talking to yourself, Rock Girl?"

Jules whipped around. Elk! He could sneak up quieter than a rabbit in a carrot patch. There he was now, leaning against the porch railing. He was smiling but his smile didn't seem to have a smile in it. She guessed she probably did the same thing now.

"No," Jules said. Then she added, feeling a little brave, "I'm talking to Sylvie." Elk nodded. Stared out into the woods. Then he surprised her by saying, "I do the same thing. Talk to Zeke. When I'm out in the woods."

It wasn't the first time Elk had come by during the day when everyone else in his own family was at school or work. Both Jules and Dad were always glad to see him. They had missed him while he was in Afghanistan. They had missed Zeke, too. Still did. But Jules could tell that no one, maybe not even Mrs Harless, missed Zeke as much as Elk did. She could tell by the smile without the smile.

Elk was living in After Zeke time.

He didn't talk much when he came by, and he never asked about school. Sometimes he brought her an interesting piece of bark or a pinecone. Not rocks, though. And that was fine by her. Rocks would have made her feel even guiltier about the twin agates she still had. He had entrusted her with them, and she had kept them safe. But what was she supposed to do with them now? She had made a promise, but she had never believed that Zeke wouldn't come home. Never. So she hadn't hunted for the Grotto that whole year — so what? Maybe it didn't even exist.

"Elk?" She waved her hand at the woods across the invisible Do Not line. "Do you think the Grotto really is out there?"

"Maybe," he said. Then he shrugged. "Maybe not."

Jules thought of all the hours that she and Sylvie and Sam had tramped through the woods, hoping for a glimpse of the mysterious cave.

"What if there's hidden treasure?" one of them would ask.

"What if there's a troll?" someone else would ask.

"What if there's a catamount?" It was always Sam who asked that one. Always, their hunts for the Grotto ended up with nothing, nothing except their determination to keep looking. With Elk next to her on the damp porch, Jules felt as though the woods were reaching out for her, as if the branches of the trees were signalling her to come towards them, as though the invisible line was daring her to step over it.

She felt a strong tug right in the middle of her stomach, as if she had her own invisible line pulling her from the porch to the woods. It caught her off guard. If she stood up, would she lose her balance? She gripped the step she was sitting on, thinking that if she let go, she might fly away.

Was this how a burning wish felt? None of her other wishes had ever felt like this. They had been small and unimportant. *Find the Grotto.* The words echoed in her ears.

Find the Grotto. As if he had read her mind, Elk tossed a pebble at her.

"You're the Rock Girl," he said, and smiled. This time there was a smile inside his smile. "If anyone can find that old cave it should be you." Then he added, "Just be careful of the bear — I've seen his tracks." What he didn't say was, *When you find it, take Zeke's rock there for me.* But that's what Jules heard in her heart.

With that, Elk was gone. He came and he went and she didn't know where or how he spent his days. She looked at the woods. The greenness of them hurt her eyes, such a thick green. And she wanted to be back in them, weaving in and out of the trees, hunting for rocks, running along the familiar paths, running to catch Syl—

The ache in her chest felt like a fist under her rib cage. The last place she had ever seen her sister was in the woods, running away from her, running to the Slip, running so fast … *so that*.

"So that what?" she said. "WHAT?"

Jules would never, ever know the answer. Just like she knew, no matter how hard she wished, no matter how much the woods beckoned her, that she would never find the Grotto if she couldn't cross her invisible line.

"Sylvie!" she yelled. Screamed. *"Sylvieee!"*

Over and over she screamed, over and over until she was screamed out. The only response was nothing, not even Dad, who must have been taking the longest shower in history.

The dampness of the porch step seeped into the back of Jules's jeans. She looked down at the Flo-Jo T-shirt. She could clearly see Sylvie running toward hers, the large yellow FLO-JO and a smiling Florence Griffith-Joyner, hands touching the track in her sprinter's crouch, like a banner across Sylvie's chest.

You take that off right now, Jules! Sylvie would have yelled. *Don't you touch my Flo-Jo shirt!*

There was a small hole in the shirt, near the hem, and she poked her finger through it. If Sylvie had been there, she would have yelled, *Don't, you'll make it bigger!* Jules pulled her finger out. She didn't want to mess up Sylvie's favourite T-shirt. She might wear it every day for the rest of her life.

15

It was time for the kits to leave the den. Their father and mother went first, up through ten metres of twisting, hard-packed tunnels. Younger Brother was next, his eyes eager and ears pricked forward, paws swift and sure. He had wanted this day since they were born.

Senna looked at Older Brother. *Hurry,* she said. She too was eager to see the above world, see what it was like and stretch her growing legs. And besides, the Someone was out there, waiting. She knew it. *Hurry,* Senna said again. But Older Brother was looking around at the walls of the den: hard dirt walls, little clumps of matted fur. The air was heavy and stale. It was time to leave, but he wasn't quite ready. He looked over at her. Senna could tell that he wanted her to go first.

So she braced with her front legs, pushed off with her hind, and up she went. A few metres up the tunnel, she paused and looked back. Older Brother stared up at her. His eyes were bright with fear.

She dipped her muzzle at him: *Come on!*

And then he was right behind her. They scrambled their way into the new world. At the entrance to the den their mother waited for them. The light was distracting – it was the first time any of them had seen sunlight – but Senna lifted her muzzle.

A thousand years of fox knowledge – the meaning of scents and sounds in the above world – beat in her bones and blood. There was a sharp nudge at her shoulder.

Tell me what you smell.

Her mother stood next to her, dark watchfulness in her eyes. Senna sniffed obediently. Her ancestors' knowledge did not fail her.

Meadow vole. Coyote. Wild turkey.

Good job, said her mother, and she turned to Senna's brothers and tested their knowledge in the same way.

In the distance, across the meadow and beyond a grove of pines, a river twinkled in the sun. *Ah!* Senna wanted, suddenly and with her entire being, to be running. *Run. Run. Run.* How fast could she run across this meadow? How long would it take her to reach the pine woods?

She stared at the woods. The Someone was there, somewhere in the thickest part of the woods. Senna knew it, just as she knew that there was an old cave there, built of rocks, one that had been there for centuries. It was ancient, perhaps as old as the grey-green bars that shimmered in the morning air, whispering to her: *Kennen*.

Then, barely metres away from Senna and Older Brother, the long grass twitched. And twitched again. Something was making its way through the meadow, something small and quiet.

Hunger leaped inside Senna's belly. She looked at Older Brother. Yes. He felt it too. They were in the above world now, ready for fresh meat. No more chewed food pushed from their mother's mouth into their own. Their parents turned to the kits and lowered their muzzles, an intent look in their eyes.

Shhh. Don't move.

Twitch. Twitch. And again, Senna kept her eyes on the twitching grass. She was the first to see the rabbit emerge. She was the first to see him freeze at the sight of the fox family. She watched his fear rise about him: an orange band that made the air itself tremble.

Her father was faster than she could have imagined.

He leaped into the air and pounced. The rabbit was in his jaws and he whipped his head back and forth three times – *SNAP!* – and the rabbit's neck was broken and limp. The father bounded back to the family and tossed the dead rabbit before them. His eyes gleamed.

Eat.

Once her belly was full, Senna breathed in long and deep.

Next, the fox parents led their kits to their new above-world home, a hollow beneath a brush pile. There was enough room for all of them to stretch against one another and keep warm in a tangle of twigs and leaves.

Younger Brother turned in a tight circle, crushing the leaves beneath him. He made a spot for himself a short distance from the rest of them. Older Brother and their parents were already asleep, soaking up the afternoon sun.

But Senna's nose filled with a scent that wasn't pine or dirt or leaves. It was familiar nonetheless. An old scent. At the same time, the cry of an unknown creature came from across the meadow, beyond the woods, almost beyond where she could hear. Though her family slept, Senna could not. The cry filled her ears and lured her from the hollow.

She flattened her paws against the cool earth and pushed up slowly, so slowly that she barely felt herself moving. When she was upright, ears pricked to the far ridge line, the cry came again. She closed her eyes, the better to hear. She sniffed, the better to know what sort of creature the sound was coming from.

Human. A human girl.

Sylvie.

Sylvie.

Sylvieeeeeee.

The grey-green bars trembled in the air before Senna as the human girl called her sadness to the sky. The weight of the sadness pressed on Senna, and she eased back into her family's nest, where she rested her head on Older Brother's neck and closed her eyes. But the human girl's cries came again, fainter now.

Who was this girl, filled with sorrow, calling and calling and calling?

16

Jules had always felt secretly ashamed of not having a burning wish the way Sylvie and Sam did. But even when she tried to think something up – and she had tried – there hadn't been anything she wanted as much as Sylvie wanted to run faster, or as much as Sam wanted Elk and the catamount to return.

Not until now.

Now she finally had her own burning wish – *find the Grotto* – and there was no Sylvie to tell.

She reached underneath Sylvie's pillow and pulled out the twin agates. Elk hadn't said one

118

word about them, but she was sure he was thinking about them. Why else would he have thought to say, "You're the Rock Girl. If anyone can find that old cave, it should be you."

Jules clicked the LED light on her hand lens and examined the agates. Even under the magnifier they were strikingly similar, which was weird for agates. Most agates were similar before they were split open, with those rough exteriors that looked like dried mud. But on the inside they were all so different, with concentric rings like the ones around Saturn or inside tree stumps, rings that made beautiful patterns. But not these two. Only tiny differences showed up under the glass.

Should she give them back to Elk now? Or should she still try to find the Grotto? What if it was near the Slip? She never wanted to see the Slip again. And there was that stinking invisible line between her and the woods, one that she wasn't supposed to cross. Something that Dad reminded her about every single day: "Not for crossing."

Dad. Dad had changed. Not in huge ways, but in ways that were big enough to be different. At night, for example, when they made popcorn and watched movies together, plenty of room on the couch now with only two of them, he sometimes put his arm around her. That was not like him, not like the dad she had known her whole life.

But everything was different in After Sylvie time, wasn't it? Maybe he kept his arm around her because, without Sylvie, he still had one free to eat popcorn with. Maybe he kept his arm around her because he was afraid that she, too, would disappear. Maybe he kept his arm around her because he didn't want her to think she wasn't his favourite. How could she be his favourite when she had let Sylvie go, and when every memory she had left of Mom grew dimmer by the day?

It had always been Sylvie who kept the memories of Mom alive. Now Dad had only his own memories. Sylvie had messed everything up.

"She slipped. She fell. You know how fast she used to run. It was an accident." Dad said it so often now that it was like a chant. The Chess Sherman chant.

"It was an accident, Juley-Jules."

"I know, Dad. I know."

The thing was, if it had been Jules who broke the Do Not that day, there wouldn't have been an accident. Because Jules wouldn't have run. She would have walked. She would have been careful. She would have stayed far back from the edge of the Slip and thrown her rock in. Everything would have been fine. Not like it was now, when nothing was fine.

Just as she clicked off the LED and stuffed the agates back under Sylvie's pillow, she heard a knock on the front door. She waited for Dad to answer it but then remembered that he had said something about cleaning out his work shed. The work shed was behind the house, not by the kitchen door.

The knock came again.

"Jules!"

Sam. Of course. Sam brought her schoolwork every day, collecting it from every teacher. It had been his idea to tell Mr Simon not to stop the bus at the Shermans' driveway any more because Jules was going to stay out of school for a while. Jules hadn't even known how much she hated seeing the bus sigh to a stop every morning until it didn't any more. And even though she also hated thinking of Sam sitting in their seat without her and Sylvie squeezed in on either side of him, she still didn't think she was ready to go back, no matter what Dad said.

Sam handed her a stack of folders, and together they stepped into the kitchen.

"We have some root beer," Jules told him. "Do you want one?"

Root beer was Sam's favourite. Jules's, too. Sylvie preferred ginger ale. *Had* preferred ginger ale. Jules reached into the refrigerator for two bottles of root beer and handed one to Sam. The pile of homework kept growing. At first she had tried to keep up, but when she showed her work to Dad, he just nodded. He didn't say, "This is Jules and Sylvie's dad, signing off." He also didn't say, "This is Jules's dad, signing off." She didn't know which was worse, to hear it or not to hear it. She plopped the homework down on the kitchen table, and she and Sam walked out onto the porch into the warm afternoon sun.

"Elk came by today," she said.

Sam nodded, frowning a little, but he didn't say anything. It was hard on him how Elk had changed, Jules knew, and she also knew that even if Sam didn't say anything about it, he worried about his brother. Maybe by letting Sam know that Elk hadn't spent the entire day alone in the woods, that he had come by the Shermans' house, visited a little bit with Jules and her dad, maybe that would make him feel better?

But Sam didn't talk about Elk. He leaned towards her as if he had a secret and whispered, "Guess what, Jules? Someone spotted a catamount."

"What?"

A hundred years had passed in these woods without even a trace of a catamount.

"There's been a sighting," he said. He smiled at her, the first real smile she'd seen from anyone in a while, and for a moment Jules felt her own face relax too.

Ever since she and Sylvie and Sam had seen that stuffed catamount at the museum in Montpelier during a school field trip, Sam had wanted to see a live one. He had stood in front of the glass case, where the cat had been mounted since 1881, and stared at it for nearly the whole rest of the visit, almost as if he were in a trance.

Jules understood — its eyes were made of glass and its coat was faded and shaggy, and she could hardly bear that it wasn't still roaming the woods and mountains, its native territory. It was hard to look at the catamount, but harder not to look at it.

"For real, Sam?" For the first time since Sylvie had gone, something that wasn't sadness or anger crept through Jules.

"Maybe he'll come here," Sam said, his voice low and soft.

"Maybe," said Jules. She knew that their woods would be the perfect place for a catamount to make a home. There were plenty of places where a large cat, even a huge one, could hide on their land. In fact, the Grotto would be a good place for a catamount to hide.

The Grotto! Her new burning wish. *Find the Grotto.*

After that day at the museum, Sam had thrown

hundreds, maybe thousands of wish rocks into the Slip: *Catamount return*. That was, until Elk left for Afghanistan. Then Sam's wishes changed to *Elk return*. Sam's wishes had been granted. Elk came home.

And now the catamount, too?

Without warning, anger zipped its way into her cheeks, small and ugly. Jules tried to clamp down on it, but she couldn't help it.

"That's so unfair!" came out of her mouth. And it was. Not fair that a catamount, the rarest of animals, had come back after a hundred years without Sylvie to see it. Not fair that a hunter or a game ranger or a scientist would probably track it down now, and, depending on who found it first, would either kill it or tranquilize it and strap on one of those radio collars. Not fair that a huge cat, a cat that could eat a person just like that, might be roaming through their woods, the woods that Sylvie once roamed through too.

And now that she, Jules, had a big, burning wish, it wasn't fair that she could never, ever throw a wish rock into the Slip again.

"It makes me so angry!" she said. "*You* make me angry! Why should both your wishes come true?"

Sam's eyes went wide. He backed out onto the porch and down the steps.

"Anyway," said Sam, his voice shaken. Jules saw that he had only wanted to share the good news with her. The small, ugly anger hovered in the air between them. She wished she could take it back, but it was already free in the world. She wrapped her arms around her waist and tried to swallow the ugliness that tasted like grit inside her mouth.

"I'll see you tomorrow, Jules," Sam said, lowering his shoulders. Then he disappeared down the drive.

Jules bowed her head. She hadn't meant to be mean, especially to Sam, who brought her homework every day, who sat and talked to her while she sorted through her rocks, who brought her new ones to add to the collection: mica and shale and talc and a triangular-shaped piece of serpentine. Super Friend Sam. She tried to get her feet to move, to run after him. But she was rooted to the bottom step.

She looked over at the invisible line. If she squinted her eyes, the greens and browns and greys of the woods boiled together, glimmered until they turned red-brown, the same colour as her sister's hair. *Why, Sylvie? Why did you want to run faster?* Jules pulled her hand back and hurled the bottle of root beer as hard as she could against the tall maple that stood next to their house. It smashed against the trunk and shattered into a thousand pieces.

"It's not fair!" she cried.

Root beer dripped down the bark of the tree. Shards of glass sparkled in the dying sun.

17

The day came when Senna's mother and father took the kits to the Disappearance. Her father led the way, her mother trotted behind the kits. As they approached the river, the smell of water grew stronger.

Slow.

Senna sensed her parents' tension. There was something here, something at the water that her parents didn't like.

Here.

The fox family gathered at the riverbank.

Their father and mother parted so that the kits could see what lay before them. Senna stared, not understanding at first. But slowly, as she watched, she saw what was happening to the bright and shining water. Here was where the tumbling, urgent flow of water fell without sign or sound into the below world. A gash in the green earth tugged the water down, and there was no more river.

Never.

The Disappearance was a place of great danger. Her mother and father turned to look sternly at their kits to reinforce their command: *Never.* The kits were never to come here. Further south, where the river re-emerged, that was all right. The river was for water and bathing and fish and prey, the little meadow creatures who came to its side. There was even a small oxbow that made a good pool for splashing.

But the Disappearance? *Never.*

The mother and father foxes stood there, stern and rigid, until they were sure that the kits understood. When they were satisfied, they turned away from the Disappearance, looking back to make sure the kits were following. *Come.* A hundred metres to the south, down the path through the woods, along the riverbank, down a bluff and then up again, the kits followed their parents. They clambered over rocks and narrowed themselves to fit beneath overhanging roots, and there it was:

The Re-emergence.

Bright water bubbled up out of the ground through a small opening surrounded by long, flat rocks. The mother and father foxes stood tall on the largest rock, their kits gathered around them. Silently they looked down. There were no predators around, so they stood in the open on the rocks, here where the river returned to the above world from its journey below.

Senna spotted a path leading away from the water, one that had been travelled by many animals. It pulled her in its direction. Older Brother nudged her with his bright black nose. *Come on.* But she ignored him, pushed him away and back to their parents. She stepped onto the path.

She trotted along it for some time, until she came to the tree line, where there was a small open glen. Not twenty metres away there was a yellow human home and a human girl.

"It's not fair!" At the sound of that voice, Senna's heart leaped. This was the same girl of the other afternoon, the girl calling her sadness to the sky. She was still filled with sorrow. And anger. This girl was all jumbled up. Sad. Angry. Both.

Senna crouched low and watched as the girl threw something, hard, against a tree. It smashed against the maple and burst into pieces, strewn around the base of the trunk. They glittered in the late afternoon light.

The girl's boots crunched on the shattered particles. She picked one up, a long, dangerous curve that looked sharp. Then she ran across the yard to the trail, close to where Senna was hiding, and threw it as hard as she could into the woods.

"You messed up, Sylvie! You ran too fast!"

The girl sank down and buried her head in her knees. Senna lowered her body to the ground and slunk forward, hidden by the growing darkness and underbrush. The crying girl's scent washed over Senna, and she breathed her in. She smelled familiar, but how? Why?

The girl was solid, not sleek like the other animals of the forest. She wore yellow cotton, a yellow cotton shirt, almost the same yellow as the humans' den. Her feet carried the scent of miles travelled in woods and fields and along the river. This girl was a creature of the woodlands, like her own fox family; Senna knew instantly the girl's family had been here a long, long time. But unlike her fox family, the girl's family was coated with a layer of sadness.

There was so much sorrow here.

Senna listened, trying to understand. She snuffed the air. A familiar scent was imprisoned in the fibres of the old cotton T-shirt draped around the crying girl. The knowledge of it was buried and faint, carried somewhere deep in her bones and her blood. She pricked up her nose and breathed in again.

Suddenly she heard the footsteps of a heavier human coming towards the girl. Senna watched. It was a male, tall and strong but also, Senna could tell, weary, exhausted.

"Come on, Jules. It's time to go in." His voice was quiet, tired.

Jules. Jules. At the sound of the word, something prickled through Senna's body. Jules. That was the name of the crying girl. Jules. The name sank into Senna's fur. Jules.

"Dad." The girl named Jules called the man Dad. Senna now knew two names. Not fox names, human names.

She watched the girl named Jules and the man named Dad walk back into their yellow home. All around her the air filled with sense and memory. Senna breathed it in. The grey-green bars trembled over her head, and all around her. *Kennen,* they whispered. A reminder.

Jules was a human girl.

And Senna was a Kennen fox.

They were linked, the two of them. Jules and Senna. But what did that mean? Senna snuffed the air again, reaching for the familiar scent. She waited in the brush, hoping that Jules would come back outside. But the yellow house was quiet.

Then she heard her mother, far away, calling her home.

Senna.

Sennnnnna.

Senna turned and ran towards the sound of her mother's voice. *Senna.* Faster and faster she ran, as fast as her legs could carry her, but not before she looked over her shoulder one more time at the yellow human house.

18

After dinner that night, Jules stacked all the papers and books that Sam had delivered to her these past weeks on top of the kitchen table. Dad shook his head at the size of the pile. "I think you need to start by sorting." Jules nodded. She was good at sorting, wasn't she? She had sorted her rock collection about a million times. But homework and rocks were two different things. She liked rocks. Loved rocks. Homework? Not so much.

"Come on, Juley-Jules," said Dad. And then, she couldn't believe it, he added, "I'm counting on you."

There it was, Jules's dad, counting on her. A small ache blossomed in the back of her throat. She swallowed hard, and then... *Kapow!*

The shot rattled the windowpane. "That was a little too close," Dad said. Jules agreed. Even though she was used to hearing the occasional gunshot, it seemed like there had been a lot of them lately.

"That bear's gotten a little too big for his britches. Seems like everyone in a three-mile radius is after him."

Most bears retreated into the woods and kept to themselves once spring came and there was food to eat – voles and rabbits and mice and mushrooms and slugs, even. But not this one. He was still out raiding bins and chasing barn cats and rummaging through the sugarhouses, where sap collected from the maple trees was boiled down into syrup. Mr Archer, the owner of Archer's Sheep Farm, was especially intent on ridding the area of the bear. He was determined not to lose even one of his sheep to it.

Kapow! Another shot, this one further away. Jules felt a rush of pity for the bear. Weren't mother bears supposed to tell their babies to steer clear of rubbish and syrup and sheep? Where *was* its mother? For a second she felt anger towards the mother bear. But then she realized that maybe the bear was just like her, without a mother, and he had forgotten everything she ever told him about being a bear.

And that led to another sorrow.

"Dad," she said. "I don't remember her."

"What are you talking about, honey?"

"Mom. You and Sylvie always talked about Mom together. Stories that you remembered."

"We did. Yes, we did."

"But I don't remember her." Her throat tightened. "I'm sorry, Dad."

Dad pulled a chair up to the table and pushed

the pile of homework to one side. Then he rested his hands palm down on the flat surface of the table and looked right into Jules's eyes. "You don't need to be sorry, honey. You were a tiny little thing when she died. I'd be surprised if you remembered anything more than a few flashes."

"But it was your ritual," she managed to gulp out. "There's no one to remember Mom with now."

"Juley-Jules," he said. "There are plenty of other rituals. Old ones, new ones. Like popcorn and a movie with my favourite eleven-year-old. That's a ritual I can get behind."

After a minute, Jules nodded. Yes. That was a ritual she could get behind too.

19

Senna was fox through and through. In the weeks since her birth, she and her brothers had grown fast, the way foxes do. She had lost most of her baby fluff and her coat was a deep auburn colour, with tips of black on her feet and nose and tail. Her mother and father guided her and her brothers in the ways of fox, ways that had been passed down for generations. A thousand years of fox knowledge soaked into Senna and her brothers.

But Senna also knew things that her brothers and parents didn't, because she was Kennen.

Unlike Younger Brother, who was linked to the wind, his element; and unlike Older Brother, who was linked to water, Senna was linked to the human girl Jules.

The day she had asked her mother about the grey-green bars that appeared sometimes, colliding soundlessly in the air around them, her mother had shaken her head.

"You are Kennen, daughter."

That was all she said. But her voice was filled with a sad wonder, and the grey-green bars appeared just at that moment. Senna stared at them, following their movements with her eyes. Her mother's eyes were on her. It was then that Senna realized her mother didn't see the grey-green bars. Her mother didn't hear the whispered *Kennen*. Her mother wasn't linked to a human, the way her daughter was, and this worried her mother.

But why?

Being Kennen made sense to Senna. She *did* know things that Older Brother didn't know, but wasn't that a good thing? She knew, for example, that the enormous cat, the one shadowing the young male human who walked through these woods, was no threat to her or her fox family. *Catamount.* He, too, had a purpose; Senna was sure of it.

20

The morning of Jules's return to school came too soon. She knew she had to go back because her father was going back to work, and she couldn't stay there all alone with just her rocks and occasional visits from Mrs Harless and Elk to keep her company. But she still... Did. Not. Want. To. Return. Not yet. There was the homework she hadn't done, for one thing. There was the school bus with Sam but not Sylvie, for another. There was the thought of all the faces that would be staring at her — or trying not to — when she walked through the big double doors,

for another. There was, there was, there was … way too much to think about.

The night before, Jules had pulled the orange mitten out of her hoodie pocket. For the millionth time, she rubbed it against her nose. Sylvie's scent was stronger in the Flo-Jo T-shirt than the mitten. The mitten smelled more of wool, lanolin. But the T-shirt held Sylvie's smell like a cup. Jules pulled the neck out and tucked her nose into the yellow cloth. Coconut. She went to sleep like that, holding the shirt against her face the way a baby held its blanket.

But the T-shirt that was such a comfort all night filled her with dread in the morning. School. Without Sylvie.

She walked to the kitchen, sat down hard and curled her toes around the rung on the kitchen chair. She used it to keep herself anchored.

"Jules," Dad said, breaking her spell. "You OK?"

She slumped down and tugged at her hair. When was the last time she had brushed it? Yesterday? Two days ago? Two weeks? She couldn't go to school with her hair in such a tangle, could she? She looked at Dad and noticed that his own hair was turning grey around his ears. The grey was something new. She tugged harder at the knot in her hair and looked at the stack of undone homework at the end of the table. A homework mountain.

She was about to tell Dad that she wasn't really OK, no, because her hair was too snarled, plus she had too much homework and she needed to sort through her rocks again, when Dad put his hand under Jules's chin and lifted it so that she had to face him. She could see the dark circles under his eyes and the way his cheeks sagged. But she also saw the firm set of his mouth.

"You can do this, Jules," he said. "You're my strong girl."

No. No, she wasn't. Not without Sylvie. The clock said almost seven, almost time to leave for school. Dad tugged on her snarled hair. "Maybe it won't be as bad as you think," he said. But how could it be anything but awful? The thought of going to school without Sylvie was unbearable. Just like the thought of playing the Maybe game without Sylvie was unbearable.

Where do you go when you die?

Maybe you grow wings.

Maybe you fly away like a bluebird.

Maybe you make yourself so small that nobody can see you at all.

21

Kennen or not, Senna was still a fox, and the lessons continued for her and her brothers. The Disappearance, the Re-emergence, hunting, fading into the woods when enemies were near. And now, the road.

If you must cross a human road, wait in the hollow beside it first. Make sure you're alone. Then cross quickly.

The mother and father foxes tested each kit. When it was Senna's turn, she paused and looked both ways, pricked her ears for noise and her nose for prey, glanced back at her parents and then trotted across. The tarmac was warm and smooth under her paws, a strange but good feeling. Once on the other side of the road, Senna and her brothers looked back at their parents, who were standing shoulder to shoulder, eyes on their kits. Relieved. Then they, too, darted across the road and into the forest.

Catamount.

The giant pale cat was closer than she had ever scented him. She looked up. There he was, stretched along the lowest branch of the maple next to her, his tawny fur almost invisible in the early morning air.

The huge cat was quiet, his muscles relaxed. Not hungry or looking for prey. *No threat.* He blinked at her. *Sister,* he said to her in the language of Kennen. *Sister.* A beautiful word.

22

Sam had told Mr Simon not to stop at the Sherman driveway. So on the day Jules went back to school, after she managed to sort of brush her hair and to stuff the homework mountain into her backpack, Dad took her to school in his pick-up truck. She was wearing Sylvie's Flo-Jo T-shirt underneath her hoodie.

"I'll call the school office to make sure you can take the bus home," Dad said while she pulled her seatbelt across her chest.

Jules stared out the passenger window as they drove the seven miles along Sumac Lane, the single-lane road that led into Hobbston and school.

Right before they crossed the bridge that spanned the Whippoorwill, from the corner of her eye she saw a flash of red zip across her vision. Fox? She twisted around to look out the back window, but the flash was gone. The woods were full of foxes, but they usually kept themselves well hidden. Jules looked back over her shoulder again, hoping for another glimmer – foxes meant luck, and she could use some luck today – but there was no sign of movement. The fox was gone.

Jules leaned hard against the truck's cloth seat. The little snow fox she had made just before Sylvie died popped into her mind. Sylvie would have loved it. She loved all the snow animals that Jules used to make for their miniature snow people, but the fox – that one would have been her favourite.

"Luck," said Dad.

"What?"

"A fox. I saw it too." He gave her a small smile. She wished she could hold on to that smile all day. But too soon, the doorways of the school loomed in front of them.

"All right, Jules," Dad said. "All right."

It was as if he was talking to himself. As if this was as hard on him as it was on her. She wished fiercely that they could just go home. Make some popcorn and sit on the couch with Dad's arm around her and watch a movie. Dad was getting out of his side of the truck and coming round to her side. But before she could put her hand on the door handle, someone else opened it.

Sam.

"Hey," he said. Then he reached behind her and grabbed her stuffed-with-undone-assignments backpack and slung it over his shoulder. Jules watched him as he raised his chin to Dad and smiled. She felt so bad for yelling at him the other day. But if Sam was still upset about it, he didn't show it.

Dad had already climbed back into the truck. She peered at him through the window, panic filling her chest. He looked back at her and winked, as if he knew how she felt. *I'll see you this afternoon,* he mouthed. The motor roared as he turned the key in the ignition. She reached for the door handle, but Sam pulled her away.

"Come on," he said, and it was her turn to nod.

"I'm OK," she said, even though she was pretty sure that wasn't true.

"I saw a fox this morning," he told her.

"I saw one too! Right before the bridge!"

"Probably the same one," Sam said, and for the first time in a long while he held out his fist and she bumped it with her own.

OK. The fox was a small, good thing. Jules took

a deep breath, and together she and Sam walked through the front doors of the school. The lockers along the hallways, the posters tacked up on the walls announcing the school play, announcing tryouts for Little League. Nothing had changed. It was all the same.

Until.

There, at the end of the hallway, was a huge poster of Sylvie at track practice, fingers brushing the ground in her sprinter's crouch, wearing the very same Flo-Jo T-shirt that Jules was wearing right now under her hoodie. Sylvie's beaming face, surrounded by signatures of their friends, by messages, looked directly at her.

Miss you.

Love you.

You were the best.

Jules felt the punch of it as it hit her full force, slammed her against the wall and pinned her there.

"Hey," said Sam. He grabbed her arm and shook it. "Jules."

"I can't do this," she said. She pressed her sleeve against her eyes, pressed the tears back. Tried to take deep breaths.

"Yes, you can," Sam said. He tightened his grip on her arm.

But how? She was here for the first time in her whole life without her sister. Jules looked down at the concrete floor of Hobbston School. She could do this. She could. One step at a time. Lockers clanged around her, opening and shutting. The first-period buzzer blared down the halls, and Sam urged her onward.

"Come on," he said. "I'll walk you to class."

Jules tried moving forward, Sam's hand on her arm.

"Come on," said Sam again. And then she heard other voices, too. Familiar voices, voices she had not heard in all this time, all calling her name: "Jules... You're back... Hey, Jules... Jules is back... Jules ... Jules ... Jules." So many friendly voices. And hugs. A whole swarm of hugs. They felt good to her, all those hugs, and they somehow helped her hold the tears back. She hadn't realized how much she'd missed being there, with all the familiar faces.

Sam stayed right by her side as they walked down the hallway and into her sixth-grade science class. The smell of rotten eggs greeted her. The science lab always smelled like rotten eggs. When she looked over her shoulder, Sam was still there.

"I'll see you after school," he said, handing over her backpack. Jules nodded to him. She turned round so that she couldn't see him walk away.

The morning went by, new and familiar at the same time. People in Hobbston, Vermont knew each other across lifetimes. Families had lived next to one another for generations. Their properties, their farms, their homesteads were practically ingrained in their bones and skin and fingernails.

Once Dad had taken Jules's left hand and turned it palm up. He had traced the shortest line that ran from her index finger to the edge of her palm.

"Here's the North River," he said. Then he traced the very thin line that crossed it, from her middle finger to her wrist. Where the two lines met, he said, "Here's Hobbston."

The longer parallel line ran beyond the first line. "Here's the Whippoorwill." Their river. The one that split their property with the Harlesses' and the Porters', the one that disappeared into the earth for a hundred metres, like a gullet, the Slip that had swallowed up her sister.

Still holding her palm up, Jules had asked him what the other line on her palm was.

"That's your lifeline, honey. Look how long it is." He smiled and traced his finger along the line. "Full of love and adventure, that's how long it is." Had he ever traced the lines of Sylvie's palm? Jules didn't know.

23

Senna and her brothers were old enough now to roam and hunt on their own. While Younger Brother preferred solitude, Older Brother and Senna liked trotting along the animal path together, playing by the river, hunting in tandem. But there was a point each day when Older Brother left Senna alone, because his fear of the catamount could not be overcome, whereas Senna was drawn to the giant cat.

They both were Kennen after all. Each day Senna watched the giant cat as he waited out of sight, alone on the cooling grass of the ridge top.

Soon enough, Elk appeared, just as he had every day since he had returned from far away.

When Elk appeared, the catamount breathed in his scent, the same way that Senna breathed in the scent of her human, Jules. Jules and Elk. Their stories were intermingled, she could tell.

But Elk's scent, and the history that it filled in, was patchy and rough. He wore the scent of trees and earth and rocks, the same as Jules, but he also wore the smell of sand and metal and black smoke, smells that he couldn't cast off, smells that clung to him like a sticky spider's web.

Senna crouched in the underbrush observing the catamount, who had hidden himself underneath the long, flat rocks that bordered the clearing as Elk approached. The clearing was anchored by a century-old oak that shaded a big rock at its base. This was Elk's sanctuary, his hideout. It was close to the cave of rocks, the one that Senna had scented on her very first day in the above world, that hidden cave that held the mingled traces of animals and humans.

Elk sank down onto the damp ground and fell back. He stretched his arms out over his head and stared up through the leaves of the tree into the early morning sky. They were next to a small oxbow formed by a curve in the river, just downstream from the Re-emergence. The catamount stayed put on the flat rocks, the same colour as his tawny coat, perfect camouflage.

Elk's scent was powerful and mysterious. It contained the scents of other humans, ones that he came across in the routine of his days. He lay still on the forest floor for a long while, and then he took a deep breath.

"Zeke?" he said, his voice quiet. "I know you're out here."

Senna watched the catamount's ears prick up. The man wasn't talking to the catamount; he wasn't talking to anything. He was just talking.

161

His voice was so low, almost a whisper, and to Senna the words themselves looked like tiny puffs of smoke when he said them. Words like *home* and *desert* and *miss* and *rocks* ... words that hung in the air and then dissolved.

The grey-green bars trembled in front of Elk. The catamount was motionless, listening.

"I miss you, brother," Elk said.

Senna was not linked to Elk, but she could still sense the pain that lived inside his strong body. She fought the urge to run away from it, to rejoin Older Brother and run – *run* – to the river and back. This pain must be far worse for the catamount, for he lowered his head and rested it on his enormous paws.

Even the sun, just emerging through the dark trees, seemed sullen, alone in its own brightness.

24

Jules was behind in every subject. That was what happened when you stayed out of school for a month. When you stopped doing homework. When you couldn't care less about school because something huge and awful had happened, something that felt so much bigger than homework ever could. She sat in her classroom and glanced at the wall, lined with books and stacks of paper and an old clock that was stuck at exactly 2.18 p.m.

At last the final bell rang, and she stuffed everything into her already stuffed backpack and stood by her locker, waiting for Sam. He had told her to, so that they could walk to the bus together. That was when Liz Redding, the second-fastest girl in school next to Sylvie, came over. Jules had known Liz since kindergarten. She swung her backpack onto her shoulder, wincing at the weight of it, just as Sam appeared beside her.

Liz looked directly at Jules. "Still no sign of the body?"

Kapow! The shock of Liz's question felt to Jules like another blow, like seeing the poster in the hallway that morning.

Liz said it again. "Still no body?"

Her sister, *a body*?

Then Jules realized that all day long the faces of her friends had been silently asking this question but no one had spoken it out loud. No one until Liz. Her words hung in the hallway air. *Still no sign of the body?*

A sharp ache jabbed Jules in her throat. She swallowed, desperate to get away and onto the bus. But Liz kept going. "I mean, don't you think it's weird that there's absolutely no sign of her? Nothing?"

"Liz!" said Sam. "Quit it!"

"What?" Liz said.

Jules began to shake. At the far end of the hall, Sylvie's beaming face glowed bright on the enormous poster. Jules shook with anger at Liz. Liz who didn't deserve to walk the same hall Sylvie had walked, Liz who had so casually referred to "the body". *The body?* Jules leaped toward Liz, fists ready. It was only because Sam jumped between the two of them that Jules didn't plough into her with fists and feet and silent rage.

Jules darted around him and then she kept on going, all the way down to the end of the hall. There she jumped straight up in the air, as high as she could, and yanked at the poster of Sylvie.

Jumped and yanked and tore at it until it hung in shreds. Until her sister was hidden, safe from the prying eyes of people like Liz Redding.

Sam was beside her not a moment later, but the poster was already ripped and crumpled and torn up.

"Come on," he said, breathless, grabbing her hand. "Come on, Jules," and he practically dragged her out of the school. There was the bus. Exhaust fumes filled their noses. Sam pulled her towards the opening door. His cheeks blazed red.

"Let's go," he said.

"But—"

Sam pushed her ahead of him. "Don't pay any attention to her," he said, his voice low and dark. "She doesn't know anything."

They walked right past their usual seat – the one that they had shared with Sylvie for years and years – to the very back of the bus. It would take them home. Jules curled into the seat by the window. There was a paper cut on the side of her hand and she rubbed it on her jeans. Liz's words tumbled around in her head, making her remember Mrs Harless's story about the beautiful boys, that stupid, stupid story about how the river had kept one brother as a prize, while many years later the other brother screamed out his terrible secret, then stepped into the river and vanished.

An image of Sylvie running and running and running flew into her head, running so fast. *Faster than a tidal wave, faster than a wind tunnel, faster than an arrow. So fast.*

So that... Sylvie's secret.

Jules leaned back against the green vinyl seat. So that what? *What?* There had to be an answer that she could figure out. Sam dug a pack of gum out of his backpack and handed her a piece. Cinnamon. Jules watched as he slowly unwrapped it and placed it in his mouth, watched the muscles in his jaw flex as he chewed. Liz's horrible question rang in her ears.

Jules sank farther down in the seat and closed her eyes. She leaned against Sam, grateful that he was right next to her.

The bus strained as it went uphill. And then it sighed as if in relief while the driver, Mr Simon, shoved the gear into neutral and let it coast down towards the bridge that crossed the river right before he pulled up to Jules's drive. As they crossed, she opened her eyes in time to look down, to look for the fox again. But there was nothing to see except the river itself.

From the road, her yellow house looked sunny in the afternoon light, the same colour as the buttercups that would appear in summer, the same flowers that were stitched on her mother's blue headband. But how could summer possibly happen without Sylvie?

The late afternoon sun agreed. In that same instant, it slipped behind a cloud and took the glow off the house. Now all it looked like was lonesome. Mrs Harless was inside, waiting for her. Dad had told her she'd be there. *Probably with more soup,* thought Jules. More quiet house. More no-Sylvie. More soup.

Mr Simon waved her forward. "Let's go, Jules," he called, not unkindly. As she stepped off the bus and onto the ground, she looked over her shoulder at Sam, waving goodbye to her from the window.

After the bus drove away and she could no longer hear the puff of its brakes, she stood alone in the driveway. The chatter of birds circled her head. The trees seemed to lean in, towards her. The warm spring afternoon filled her lungs. And all around, the green, green, green of spring rushed towards her. She turned her face to the sky.

Where do you go when you die?

Maybe you turn into wind.

Maybe you turn into stars.

Maybe you turn into a firefly and light up the night.

Jules dropped her backpack on the driveway. She looked across the yard. Her father would be home soon.

But then she turned towards the woods. There was the invisible line. Despite the greyness all around, it shimmered in the dim light. If she ran as fast as she could, faster than a cheetah, faster than a thoroughbred, faster than a hornet, she could cross it. And then she would be in the woods again, the woods that she and Sylvie loved. Elk went there every day, to a clearing, he had told her.

"I go there to talk to Zeke," he'd said. "It's weird, but somehow it feels like he's near by."

He had shrugged. "You talk to Sylvie, I talk to Zeke," he'd said. "I don't care what others would say if they knew. Some things don't make sense to anyone but yourself."

Jules wanted to be back in the woods. She wanted to sit with Elk in the clearing. She wanted to see if she could spot the little fox again, if she were quiet and sneaky enough not to startle it first. She wouldn't mind seeing the bear, either. He was so fat and happy from all the food scraps he'd been stealing that he probably wouldn't even notice her. Yes, it was time to get back to the woods.

And now, her brand-new burning wish — *find the Grotto* — tugged at her.

She took a step. Then another. But the invisible line stopped her. She stood as still as she could so as not to make any noise, not a sound, and then she inched forward. Her toes were right up against it. It would be so easy to cross. It was invisible, after all. Jules leaned forward. She could do it. One step, and she would be over it. She felt the pull, as if there were a rope tied around her waist and the woods themselves were tugging on it. She could almost feel the rope's rough, scratchy braids in her palms. An invisible tug-of-war.

She nudged the line again with her toe. There was no fence, no wall. But it would mean another broken Do Not. Her whole life, she and Sylvie had been allowed to roam through the woods together with Sam. So long as they stayed away from the Slip, and within earshot of the house, so long as they didn't mess with any wild animals, they could tramp around to their hearts' delight.

But they had broken the cardinal rule: *Do not, under any circumstances, go near the Slip.* And because of that, Sylvie was gone, and now she and Dad lived in a time called After Sylvie. Jules reached into her pocket and pinched her sister's mitten, hard. If only Jules had held on tighter, if only she had gone with Sylvie. She could have caught her, she would not have let go. She would not have been like the River Brothers. She would have held on tight.

Do not cross that line, Dad had said. He had added, *Don't even think about it.* Right on time, Jules heard the familiar rumbling of her father's pick-up. He pulled into the drive and slammed the door of the cab and walked towards her, her tall, worried dad, his arms outstretched.

"Juley-Jules," he said. "We did it. We made it through the first day back."

And for a brief moment, the thought of stepping over the line let go its terrible grip.

25

K*apow!*

The windowpane in the Porter kitchen rattled. The crack of gunfire always surprised Sam, even though he had grown up hearing it. Someone must be out for that stupid bear again. Unless it was wild turkey season already. Sam had lost track. Then he remembered that his father had had a call from Fred Archer. "He's worried about his lambs," he'd told Sam, stuffing his phone in his front pocket. Then he looked right at Sam and said, "Archer won't come onto our property, but you be careful out there anyway.

Bears don't care about property lines." Then he sighed. "And sometimes an angry farmer won't either."

Sam knew that was true, even though he'd never seen anyone trespass on their property, or the Shermans', either. He knew that the Whippoorwill was a better barrier than any fence.

Kapow! There it was again.

Sam knew the sound must upset his brother, reminding him of the war he had come home from. He could tell by the way Elk's eyes squinted, the way his shoulders tensed up, whenever he heard it.

Between Jules and her crazy anger at Liz, and Elk and his silence, Sam was exhausted. Sometimes he wanted to shout that *he* missed them too. He, Sam Porter, had loved Sylvie and Zeke! But there was no room for his sadness, smushed between Elk and Jules the way he was.

Maybe things would begin to change now,

though. Jules might have gone nuts today at school, but he couldn't really blame her. Liz was an idiot. And Jules was back. He didn't have to sit on the bus alone any more.

And at dinner that evening, Elk had suddenly looked up and said, "I've got the strangest feeling that someone's watching me out there in the woods." Before anyone could reply, a look of embarrassment came over Elk's face and he added, "It's probably that bear that's been getting into everyone's bins."

Maybe, thought Sam, *but what if it's the catamount?* He had listened to the news on the radio every morning but there had been no more reports.

The old catamount in Montpelier had done something to him. Ever since he had seen him, since he had stared at that case and seen his glass eyes, he had longed to see a real one, as if seeing one alive might restore the dignity of the one in the glass case. It mattered, didn't it? Seeing one that wasn't trapped, or at least knowing for sure that one was still out there. It mattered.

Kapow!

Another shot. This one closer. Sam pushed his chair away from the table. If there really was a catamount in their area, would a hunter shoot something so rare? Dumb question. If Fred Archer thought that his lambs were in trouble, it wouldn't matter. Even if it was against the law, that catamount would not be allowed to live.

Sam understood the farmer's point of view — he had to protect his livestock. But just as there were rogue bears out there, there were also rogue hunters, hunters who would get it into their heads that a catamount rug for the living room was a good idea. Sam knew they wouldn't care if this was the last catamount in the world.

But what if it was? What if his catamount was the very last one? The thought of there being only one of the big cats left made Sam fiercely protective. He pictured the small red fox, the one beside the bridge. She would be just as much a target. Foxes were not beloved by people who raised lambs either. It was a hard balance to maintain, between the humans who lived next to the woods of Vermont and the wild animals who roamed within them. To Sam, they were all woodland creatures. Every last one.

PART THREE

26

Senna awoke when the roosters at the farm across the river began to crow. Far to the east, a line of light began to rise above the pines. Older Brother was still sleeping. She pushed her muzzle into his neck experimentally, to see if he was ready to wake up, but no.

She hated being apart from him, but her need to find the Someone had grown stronger and stronger. She was linked to the girl Jules, but there was still a Someone she was supposed to find. It was a need that started in her gut and radiated into all four of her paws. The grey-green bars shimmered in the corner of her vision. Now, in the early morning, the river called to her. Maybe the Someone was there, by the river. She brushed against her sleeping brother once more, and then off she went.

Past the clearing, with its scent of Elk and catamount. Past the smell of the yearling bear and his stench of human rubbish. Past the hidden cave with its mingled scents: humans both ancient and recent, animals and rocks.

Senna's heart thudded in her chest. She lifted her head and saw that she was nearly there, bright sparkles of water ahead. She began to slow, trotting down the animal path that skirted the riverbank, leaping lightly over rocks and roots, through the piles of boulders and leaves, until she stood on a high, flat ledge above the Re-emergence.

She looked down. The water came bubbling up out of the darkness, spreading over the surface of the earth, singing and murmuring its way south. She was distracted by a new scent, unfamiliar and tantalizing. Not prey. Senna scrabbled with her paws and claws, shoving aside smaller rocks with her muzzle.

There.

A small, dirty circle of cloth, human cloth. Had it once been blue? Black? Whatever its original colour, it was faded now, by the sun and the snow and the elements. Mud-streaked, with claw marks.

Senna bent her head and sniffed. Happiness rushed through her at the scent. She plucked it up between her teeth and shook her head so that the little band of cloth snapped back and forth. Then she smelled something else in the cloth, something that commanded all her attention.

It reminded her of something, but what?

Whiteness rose in Senna's vision.

White. Cold. Clean.

Snow.

In the knowledge passed down by her fox ancestors she knew all about snow, even though she had never felt the crunchy cold of it beneath her paws. She breathed in the strip of cloth. Then she plopped into the fallen leaves beside the water and rested her head on it.

The ancient memory of falling whiteness made her shiver. But then she saw something else, something that wasn't ancient at all. A snow family. There was a mother and a father and two daughters. And right in the middle, a tiny snow fox.

Jules. Jules had made the small fox.

Then there were footsteps, running out into that cold clean snow. Senna could feel it in her own body, in her own legs, the sensation of running through falling whiteness.

Senna's whole body buzzed. There was something she was supposed to do with this narrow band of cloth, faded blue, the blue of almost-day, with stitched-on flowers.

She shook the band again and picked up her pace. First she crossed the field, then she headed directly towards the cave of rocks, the one behind the enormous white pine, just off the path.

Senna paused. The scent of humans was strong here. So was the scent of catamount, and a dozen other animals who lived near by. But there was something else, too. The scent that she smelled on the band of cloth was also here, in the hidden cave. Slight, but there nonetheless. Senna hesitated. She understood that not every creature in the woodlands could see the cave, and even fewer could enter. Or would enter. The cave made itself known only to those with a reason for finding it. With the cloth in her mouth, Senna had a reason.

She nosed aside the drooping leaves and edged her way inside, where she leaned into the darkness, waiting for her eyes to adjust.

This was an old, old place, a place where many before her had come, both human and animal. And Kennen, too. As if to prove it, the grey-green bars swayed before her, glimmering in the darkness. The Kennen. This was Senna's home territory. She breathed in the ancient smells, both familiar and not.

A sensation of warmth, of quiet, filled her, and she remembered the den of her birth, far below the surface of the earth. The grey-green bars slipped in and around her; then they banged together silently against the cavern walls. They threw off a spark of light, tiny at first, then growing in size. While Senna watched the light expand, a woman appeared inside it, a woman with long hair the same colour as Senna's own fur, reddish-brown now that she was almost full-grown, flickering in and out.

Oh! Senna knew her immediately. It was her!

The Someone. At last.

Joy sparkled through Senna from the tip of her nose to the end of her long tail. She stood on her hind legs and pressed her paws against the Someone's legs. She had found her! The missing Someone. Senna turned in a tight circle; a tail-chasing happiness filled every part of her small fox body. The colliding bars seemed to chime.

But then the woman turned her back to Senna and began to walk away. Senna followed. Where was she going?

Deeper into the cave the woman with the red-brown hair led her. But the woman did not turn around. Senna trotted faster to keep up, the band of cloth in her teeth.

Senna heard a woman's voice, familiar but not. *Danger, Senna. You will need to run fast, as fast as you can.*

Senna ran, but she couldn't keep up.

The woman grew smaller and smaller. *Run*

faster, Senna. But no matter how fast Senna ran, she couldn't catch her. Faster and faster she went, so fast, as fast as a fox could go. But it wasn't fast enough. Finally the woman disappeared, and all the happiness Senna had felt evaporated into the stale air of the cave. Only the woman's words remained, echoing in Senna's ears. A message. Danger was near by, danger was coming.

Run faster, Senna.

But Senna didn't want to run, she wanted to stay with the woman, she wanted to curl up on her lap, wanted to go to sleep there. Senna tried to follow her again, but the woman was nowhere.

A whimper escaped her. The bars flickered once, and then they also disappeared. The band of cloth lay on the beaten dirt floor of the cave, and Senna plucked it up between her teeth and re-emerged into the sun.

Then the fur on the back of her neck rose. The

hunter was out there, his rifle strapped to his back. The woman's message rang in Senna's ears. *Danger. You will need to run fast, Senna.*

But first, Senna knew, she had to find Jules. She had to give the headband to Jules.

27

Jules managed to make it through another day of school, although each time she saw Liz Redding, her jaw tightened. Even the bus ride home with Sam didn't help to tamp down her anger. When Mr Simon dropped her off, she stormed down the steps.

"Are you OK, Jules?" Sam called from the bus window. But she didn't have an answer. She didn't know if she was OK or not. She just knew that she was tired of being trapped in After Sylvie. As she headed towards the house the invisible line glowed, almost as if it were taunting her. *Do not. Do not. Do not.*

She walked into the house and let the door slam behind her, then let her heavy backpack thud onto the table. She was about to stomp through the house, but Mrs Harless called, "Jules! Can you keep it quiet?"

In the living room, all the curtains were closed. The room was too dark. And Mrs Harless was too pale.

"One of my migraines came on this morning," Mrs Harless told her. "I'm just going to lie here on the sofa for a bit."

"Sorry," Jules whispered. And she was for a moment, but then she wasn't, because there, in the dark living room, she saw a chance. She waited until she was sure Mrs Harless was asleep, and then, quieter than falling snow, Jules slipped out the front door and turned towards that invisible line and walked directly up to it. She looked around to make sure no one was there, and then she spoke aloud to the woods.

"Dad," she said, "I know this is against the rules."

Then she stopped. Hearing the words out loud – and knowing how adamant her dad was about this new Do Not – made her hesitate. She looked around again, double-checking that she was alone.

"But hear me out," she said. "I need to find this place. I made a promise to Elk and I didn't keep it…" She stopped again. She wasn't making much sense.

"I won't go anywhere near the –" she made herself say it – "the Slip. I promise."

There. That would have to do. Before she lost her nerve, she stepped over the invisible line and onto the trail. Liz Redding's question streamed through her head: *No sign of the body?* No one had found Sylvie's body. No one.

But Elk had told her that he thought Zeke's

spirit was in these woods. Maybe Sylvie's spirit was there too. It was the last place that Sylvie had been, in the woods, after all. If Jules couldn't find her sister's body, maybe she'd find her spirit. Maybe she'd find it in the Grotto. It was a place of spirits, at least that was what Mrs Harless said. And Elk believed it, otherwise he wouldn't have given her the twin agates to place there in case the worst happened.

Jules looked up, way up, at the tall feathery tops of the white pines, dark against the sky. The bus journey home had taken for ever. She guessed that it was about four thirty. She had to hurry. Dad would be home soon. She picked up her pace, veering left after the stand of white birch, past the giant white pine. As she got deeper into the trees she could smell the water from the river. It was a familiar, fresh smell. She had not been near the Whippoorwill since Sylvie had vanished. She wasn't going there now. She never, ever wanted to see the watery gorge again.

Jules kept the sound of the river to her right and soon came upon the oxbow. This was a shallow pool, an offshoot of the river, and it usually dried up in the summer months. But in the spring it was filled with melted snow and rainwater, perfect for animals to pause for a drink or for a migrating duck to stop over for a day or two. Jules and Sylvie and Sam had always gone to the oxbow in spring, crouching in the brush, trying to be woodland creatures so that they wouldn't scare away the fawns and does and foxes and raccoons.

Jules stepped towards the shallow pool, but as she did, the unmistakable sound of an engine filled the air.

A four-wheeler.

She peered through the branches. The four-wheeler drew up beside the edge of the oxbow and the driver swung himself off in a single easy motion.

Elk! Of course.

Jules started to call to him but stopped. Seeing Elk in the woods was different from having him stop by the house. There was something about him that made her think he had come here to be alone. Jules crouched low behind the trees and stayed still.

Elk reached behind the seat and pulled something out, a long leather case that zipped on one side, and inside it … a gun. Before Jules could even blink, Elk brought the gun to his shoulder and fired.

Boom. Boom. Boom.

The sound slammed into her.

Boom. Boom. Boom.

Jules's heart skipped a beat. A flock of starlings scattered through the tree limbs, muffling her whimper. She pressed her hand over her mouth to keep herself quiet. Elk reloaded and shot again. Now Jules covered her ears, but it didn't help.

Boom. Boom. Boom.

The shots resonated through the ground and up through the soles of her boots. A squirrel skittered by, a blur of brown-and-grey fur. Smoke filled her nostrils. She counted the shots in her head. Nine so far.

Boom. Boom. Boom.

Ten, eleven, twelve. Elk kept reloading and firing again. Slower now.

Boom.

Boom.

Boom.

Jules squatted down and pressed her forehead against her knees, her hands over her ears. The air around her crackled with each shot.

Boom. Boom. Boom. Boom. Boom.

And then there was one more, the last. *Boom.*

Twenty-one shots across the water. A deep quiet now settled over the woods. Elk gently lowered the gun and stood as silent as a stone.

After a long time he put his hand over his heart and called out, "That's for you, Zeke." Then he swung the gun over his head three or four times and hurled it into the water. *Splash*. Elk watched it sink, and then he saluted. Jules saw how crisp the salute was, how sad Elk's face was. Then he turned round, climbed back on the four-wheeler and drove off.

The echo of the gunfire was all around, the air sharp with the smell of sulphur from the spent ammunition.

Shame crept through Jules. She felt as if she had just witnessed something private. Something too private, something that was intended for no one but Elk and Zeke.

She rose, but she couldn't walk away just yet. Her legs were shaky and she felt a little dizzy. The stream of light from the sun acted like a spotlight on the edge of the water. She followed its beams and stepped forward, and there, right next to the shore, partly covered by leaves and branches, was a paw print the size of a dinner plate.

Jules squatted down and balanced on her toes. Hesitantly, she reached out to it. Her fingertips came right to the edge of the track. She pulled her hand back, fast.

Catamount.

It could be nothing else.

Sam! His burning wish! And almost instantly the huge cat in the glass case at the museum loomed in front of her vision. She could see its vicious teeth and the wide paws, paws that sheathed long, thick claws, claws that could rip through the skin of its prey. Suddenly she couldn't make her muscles move. What if the catamount was just behind her, waiting to sink his claws into her? *You have to go,* she told herself, and finally she managed to look up.

There, only a few metres in front of her, was a fox.

28

The loud booms of gunfire terrified Senna. Band of cloth clutched in her jaws, Senna had tracked Jules to the oxbow. She was followed by Older Brother, who had traced his sister's scent through the woods. Reluctant though he was to be that close to any human, he was more reluctant to leave Senna. When the tall man with the rifle started shooting, Jules sank to her knees and the two foxes melted into the underbrush behind her. Then they waited, waited and waited along with Jules, until the noise finally soaked into the ground and the chittering of a hundred birds filled up the woods.

Senna crept forward, onto the path. Brother hovered in the background, watching, wary. Senna stood motionless, the narrow strip of cloth clutched between her teeth, while Jules rose to her feet. Her bright hair swung about her shoulders as she made her way to the oxbow and knelt down. Senna and Older Brother heard her gasp and watched as she leaned forward and hovered her spread fingers above the catamount print.

Senna placed one paw after another on the grass, dry in the late afternoon, smelling of green. She carried the cloth band between her teeth.

Another step.

Jules was still kneeling by the giant paw print.

Senna did not move, even when the girl stood and turned. Spine straight and ears pricked up, she met the girl's gaze. The two of them — fox and girl – looked at each other and did not blink.

Senna lowered her head to the ground and let the narrow band of cloth slip from her mouth. In the same moment, she melted back into the tall grass where Older Brother waited. She crouched low, retreating deeper. Jules pounced like an animal on the dirt-crusted once-blue band. She held it to her nose and breathed in.

If Senna had been alone she would have stayed. But Older Brother had had enough of humans. He stood over her, batting at her with his paw. The smell of catamount was strong now, too, much stronger than before. He nudged her with his muzzle, panic in his touch and eyes. He barked, and finally he pulled her by the ruff of her neck, and they were off.

29

Sylvie's headband! The same headband she'd been wearing when – when. Jules dashed that thought away and turned to the next one. Had a fox just *given* her the headband? Wait, a *fox*? Could that have just happened? And if it *had* happened, where had the fox got it? Her mother's headband, the blue one with the yellow buttercups embroidered on it. The same headband that Sylvie had worn the day she disappeared.

Liz Redding's terrible question came back in that moment. *No sign of the body?* Because this *was* a sign of the body, wasn't it? Sylvie had been wearing this when she fell into the Slip. This was a part of Sylvie, come back.

Jules's thoughts were all jumbled up. Had that little fox really been standing there just now? Had it really dropped the headband right in front of her? Why wasn't the fox afraid of her – was it rabid? No, it wasn't rabid. It was a fox who had come to give her a gift. No, foxes didn't give gifts. Foxes weren't human. Foxes were afraid of humans. They avoided them. None of this made any sense.

But the headband made sense. The headband was real. It was Sylvie's. Their mother's. Sylvie's. It had belonged to both of them.

Jules rubbed her fingers over it. Faded grey now, only a remnant of the blue it had once been. Sylvie had always taken such good care of it, washed it by hand in the sink, cold water only, using her coconut shampoo instead of detergent. Jules held it up to her nose and breathed it in.

Dirt. The dirt of her woods. And the river, the Whippoorwill. The slightest scent of Sylvie's coconut shampoo. Dirt. Snow. River. Coconut. The headband held all those smells. But it also had a smell that Jules didn't recognize. Not at first. She breathed in again.

Fox. It must be fox. The little red fox that had stood there looking right back at her, no fear in her eyes or in her posture, as if she had been waiting for Jules to notice her so that she could give her the headband and then fade away.

Foxes were supposed to bring luck. But Jules did not feel lucky at all.

She pulled her hand lens out from under her T-shirt. Then she rubbed one of the embroidered flowers with her thumb until some of the silt let go, showing the yellow threads below. She clicked on the LED beam and shone it on the faded buttercup. In the light's glow it was just as bright yellow as the mustard that had splashed out of the jar that day her mother had crumpled in half on their front steps. As bright as it was in Sylvie's hair the day she ran down the trail, ran so fast, away from Jules.

30

From the shadows of the trees, Senna watched as Jules stood up, the headband encircling her wrist. For a moment Jules seemed disoriented, bewildered. But then she collected herself and took off in the direction of the tree line. With Older Brother by her side, Senna resisted the urge to follow the human to the yellow den. He reached over and tugged on the scruff of her neck. He nipped at her nose and chewed on her ears.

She batted at him with her paw. *Danger, Senna. You have to run fast.* The Someone's voice was still in her ears. But for now the danger seemed past. The gunshots that had rung out earlier were done. The bear was not on the move. Most importantly, she had delivered the gift to Jules.

She gave herself a whole-body shake, stretched and leaped after her brother. Her beautiful Older Brother. She glanced at the huge sand-coloured cat, only a few metres away, as she ran past him. He blinked his yellow eyes and rested his paws on his chin.

31

Sam walked up his drive and there was Elk, waiting for him just like the other day. This time, however, he took him by the arm and said, "Come with me. I want to show you something." Elk's voice sounded different to Sam. Instead of the almost-whisper that he had been speaking in these past weeks, now his words tumbled out, crisp and clear, sounding like the old Elk, the one Sam had grown up with.

Sam grinned. It was unusual enough that his brother had been waiting for him, but this, this was so unexpected that Sam just dropped

208

his backpack at the door and followed Elk into the woods. The sun hung from the branches of the trees as if the trees had snagged it on its way down, slowing its descent into the spring evening. It would be dark soon.

"Hurry up, Sammy," Elk said. Sam hadn't heard that nickname since way back in the days when Elk and Zeke used to let him tag along on their expeditions.

Sam picked up his pace, and soon he realized that they were aiming for the oxbow. The river was slower there, and muddy. It was a gathering place for animals, so Sam and Sylvie and Jules used to go there to hide behind the foliage and watch the comings and goings of their fellow woodland creatures. It was a little swampy and usually swarming with mosquitoes. Sam didn't care about that, though. He just wanted to keep walking with his brother beside him.

"What is it?" asked Sam.

"You'll see."

Elk set a steady pace, not too fast, not too slow. Was this the kind of pace they set in the army? Sam wanted to ask, but instead he just kept walking. He pushed his hand down deep in his pocket. A few minutes later and they were there, on the bank at the curve in the river.

"Look," Elk told him, pointing down.

Sam did. The water was quiet and still in the late afternoon. He couldn't see too far beneath the surface. Mostly what he noticed was the wavy reflection of the tall trees all around them, a few evergreens, and others just getting their new spring leaves. There were a handful of geese on the far bank, likely new arrivals from the south. But Sam didn't think Elk had brought him here to see geese.

"What am I looking for?"

"You'll know when you see it. Keep looking."

Sam kept looking. Paw prints. Deer. Raccoons.

And then ... wait ... waitwaitwaitwaitwait! ... there was no mistaking it. "Yes!" Sam sprang straight up and barrelled down to the edge of the water. All his life he had waited for the catamount to return, and now, here he was!

Elk jumped down off the ledge and landed beside him, and Sam leaped right onto his brother's back, knocking both of them to the ground, Sam laughing and shaking his head. Elk grinned back.

"Looks like those wish rocks worked," said Elk.

"I can't wait to show Jules and Syl—" Sam caught himself. "Jules, I mean." A small bit of happiness leaked out with the mistake of it. But not all of it. Sam looked up at the tall trees. Wouldn't Jules think this was a good thing? Wouldn't the proof of *Catamount return* count as a good thing?

But then he remembered the day she'd got

so angry at him. And he couldn't really blame her. It *wasn't* fair that he had got both his wishes and Jules – well, Jules... Elk reached over and put his hand on top of Sam's head and rested it there.

"I know," Elk said. "I know."

And he did know, thought Sam, of course Elk knew. He had lost Zeke, just like Jules and Sam had lost Sylvie.

"The thing is," Elk said, "sometimes I feel like Zeke is still out here, like he's watching me. If that's true, then who's to say that Sylvie isn't out here too?"

Sam pushed himself up off the ground. Elk was right. Who was to say? They both dusted themselves off and knelt back down to examine the gigantic print. Elk put his hand over it. It was almost an exact match.

"Grandma Harless used to tell us about special animals," said Elk, "spirit animals – she said they

212

were born into the world to help some other being."

"Help how?"

"Don't know. She didn't either. She said it was beyond our knowing, something only the spirit animals knew. 'Beyond our ken' was what she said."

Then Elk moved aside and let Sam put his hand inside the catamount print. His hand wasn't that much smaller than Elk's any more. A catamount! He could hardly believe it. And here they were, in the exact spot where the catamount had been. His second burning wish had come true. First Elk had come home, and now the catamount had returned. All those wish rocks.

"Did Zeke have a burning wish?" Sam asked his brother.

"Yeah. One."

"What was it?"

"To come home to these woods."

32

When Jules got back to the house, she was relieved to see that Mrs Harless was still asleep on the sofa. A small twinge of guilt passed through her. If Mrs Harless had seen Jules cross the invisible line, she surely would have called Dad and he'd be here already.

Jules looked at the clock above the sink. It was almost five thirty. Dad would be home any minute. She ducked into her bedroom and tucked the headband underneath her pillow, just in time to hear Dad's truck rumble up the drive. After he gave Mrs Harless a ride home – her hand over her eyes to keep out the sun – he stood in the doorway of Jules's room.

"Got something for you," he said, both hands behind his back. "Guess which one."

This was the trick he had played on them when they were little, shifting the object, whatever it was, from one hand to the other. She pointed, and he held his closed fist out to her. She pried it open. On his palm lay a polished chunk of verde antique, dark green with lacy white lines tracing the surface of the serpentine.

"That's *beautiful*," Jules said. "Where did you find this?"

"At a construction site, if you can believe it. I saw it and thought of my rock girl. My strong-as-a-rock girl."

Jules closed her fingers over the serpentine. It was still warm from Dad's hand. It might have made a good wish rock, even though Jules knew she would never add it to the striped sock in her closet. Not this one.

Wish rocks.

Had Dad ever had a burning wish? She must have had a strange look on her face, because he tilted his head at her questioningly. She decided to ask him outright.

"Dad, did you ever have a burning wish?"

He smiled. "I used to," he said. "I had two, in fact. When I fell in love with your mom, I had a burning wish that she would love me back. And then we both had a burning wish to have children."

"But … Mom and Sylvie are gone now."

He shook his head. "Doesn't matter, Jules. What matters is that I had two burning wishes, and they both came true."

He reached out and wrapped both his hands around the one of hers that was holding the chunk of serpentine. "And that makes me a lucky, lucky man."

There was something in his voice that was quiet and true. She decided to think about it later. This new piece of serpentine would need its own spot. Maybe on the windowsill. Not under the pillow next to Sylvie's headband. She wasn't ready to tell Dad about the headband yet. Plus, how could she – he'd want to know where she got it! So she tossed the serpentine from hand to hand until he went to the kitchen to start dinner.

But when she set the rock on the windowsill, it didn't seem to belong there, either. Nor did it fit with the other rocks on the top of her bookshelf. She didn't want to put it in her Christmas box of rocks, because it might get jumbled up in there.

She opened her left palm, and with her right hand placed it squarely in the centre. She felt the weight of it, the heft. She curled her fingers over it. It was warm from being handled. And old. So old. Jules knew that her rocks had been here for aeons, maybe from when the Earth first formed. They'd been around since before the Abenaki and the Norse settlers, since before the mastodons and the woolly mammoths and the cave lions. Before all that.

Cave lions.

The word *cave* brought the Grotto to her mind. Hadn't Mrs Harless told them that it had been a memorial, that for centuries people had taken rocks there to honour their dead? She thought about Elk and his twenty-one shots. She knew that it was his way of honouring Zeke.

Jules *had* to find the Grotto. Elk had honoured Zeke with his twenty-one-gun salute, and finding the Grotto and placing the perfect rock there would be her way of honouring Sylvie.

I got your back, sister.

She would have to cross the line again. Just this one last time. She might not be able to do it tomorrow, or even the next day. She would have to wait for the right opportunity. And while she didn't wish for Mrs Harless to get a migraine every day, she sort of wished that she'd at least get sleepy and want to take a nap. That didn't make her a horrible person, did it?

Besides, she would only break the one rule — she would still stay within earshot of the house, she would still not go to the Slip. The only rule she would break would be the one about the invisible line.

And another thing. When she found the Grotto she would return the twin agates to Elk, no matter how much she loved them, so he could do the same for Zeke. With great care, Jules set the verde antique rock on her bedside table.

Sam's wishes had come true. Dad's wishes had come true. Even Sylvie's wish to run faster had come true, in a way. Hers would too.

33

The message had been given to Senna by the Someone — *danger, Senna* — and she was on alert. In the days and weeks after finding the headband she kept returning to the old cave. She sniffed the dirt floor and scratched at the hard walls but the Someone never reappeared. Senna called in her fox voice, whimpered for her. Where was she? And why didn't she come?

The grey-green bars shifted in the air around her. *Run, Senna. Run faster.* And Senna did. Her sturdy legs grew muscular and strong as she raced through the forest. She sought out the catamount

as he shadowed his human, the man named Elk. She scented the whereabouts of the foolish young bear, who was still out there stealing human food, moving from one dustbin and farm to another.

She ran along the banks of the Re-emergence. She ran through the pines all around her. And every day she ran to the edge of the clearing and waited for the sun to begin its descent. That was when she was most likely to see Jules.

Maybe, thought Senna, if she could lead Jules to the cave then she might find the Someone again. Maybe Jules was the key? Maybe.

Senna waited underneath the old wooden bridge each afternoon. Cars and trucks rumbled over the thick wooden planks but Senna stayed hidden until she could hear the sigh and groan of the school bus. Then she scampered up the gravelled bank to wait in the tall grass as the bus lumbered past. Jules's face would be in the very last window, peering out. Would Jules see her?

Sometimes yes, sometimes no.

But on the yes days, her bright eyes behind the window flashed light down at Senna. Jules. When Jules got off the bus she usually walked right up to the trail that led to the Disappearance. Then she stopped. Sometimes Jules was aware of Senna's presence, sometimes not. It was almost as if they were playing a game of hide-and-seek with each other.

But Senna wasn't really playing games. She wanted Jules to follow her, wanted Jules to help her find the Someone again. Day after day, Jules left her house and walked right up to the beginning of the trail that led into the woods, and day after day, she stopped.

Sometimes Older Brother came with Senna, but she knew he didn't like being so close to the humans. *It's against our fox nature,* he said. Senna knew that was true, but she also knew that while she was fox, she was also Kennen, which was something that Older Brother didn't understand. So more and more often she came alone, hiding and seeking, waiting for Jules to step onto the trail. But day in, day out, she walked only to the edge. Nothing changed.

Until the day Senna smelled something besides the familiar scents of Jules and the T-shirt she always wore.

Bear.

And a human, following the bear.

Danger, Senna. Run faster.

Just then, as Senna's heart began to beat faster – *danger, Senna* – Jules walked up, almost on top of her.

34

Hello, little fox," Jules said. "Were you waiting for me?"

Maybe it was weird, talking to a wild animal, but she couldn't help it. Besides, she kept running into this same fox, the fox who'd had Sylvie's headband. The sight of her felt like huge good luck, especially right now. Jules was taking a chance. Mrs Harless was back in the house in the living room, reading a book. All these days, Jules had been patient, waiting for her chance, waiting and waiting and waiting, and finally she couldn't wait any more.

A person could explode if they thought about something too hard, couldn't they? Hadn't she read that somewhere? And finding the Grotto was all she could think about. So she waited for Mrs Harless to settle onto the sofa, waited to hear the turns of the pages, counted to one hundred to see if Mrs Harless was going to put the book down or keep reading. At the end of one hundred, Mrs Harless kept right on going. It must be a good book. Jules grabbed the twin agates, the green serpentine that Dad had given her and her mother's headband.

She jumped right over the invisible line. She had to hurry. Dad would be home soon.

And then, luck! Right in front of her was the fox, almost as though it were waiting for her. Jules bent down, taking precious seconds, and spoke softly so that she wouldn't scare it away.

"Hello, little fox." The fox sat down, waited, ears pointing straight up. Jules paused. *Do not mess with wild animals*. It was one of her father's Do Nots. But her father had also said that a fox was lucky. Shouldn't that count too? Jules knelt down and held out her hand. The fox stayed still. She met Jules's eyes with her bright, steady gaze.

The sun slanted down through a gap in the pines and landed on the fox's fur, lighting it up. She looked up at Jules, turned and began to trot down the path, then paused and looked back. Did she want Jules to follow her?

At first the fox just trotted along the trail, making it easy for Jules to keep up, but then she picked up her pace. Jules thought she might have scared her, so she tried to slow down, to put some distance between them. The fox would then wait, and as soon as Jules almost caught up, she sped up again.

It was crazy, but the little fox seemed to be leading her somewhere, towards something. Jules followed. They made their way down the path, the fox a few metres ahead of Jules, in the direction of the Re-emergence. Then the fox ducked into the underbrush beyond an enormous white pine and disappeared.

Where was she?

Jules had never ventured off the path at this particular place before. The white pine was so huge that it had obscured a tall outcropping of mossy rocks. Vermont was a land of rocks and trees. Like snowflakes, no two rocks ever looked the same – the exception being the twin agates that Elk had given her. The rocks hidden behind the white pine, however, were each similar in size and sat in a neat row, resting one on top of the other.

Where was the fox? Jules turned in all directions, craning for a glimpse. She had lost her. But then she took a step back and looked hard at the straight, neat line of rocks. What she saw next was a small opening into and through a curtain of brush that nearly hid an archway of stones, the opening about the size of her shower door.

She began to tremble.

All these years. All the times she and Sylvie and Sam had roamed through these woods. They must have passed this way dozens of times and never seen it, blocked as it was by the giant pine, a pine they had passed a million times. But now, in the waning moments of daylight, Jules knew exactly what she was looking at. The Grotto was right in front of her. And without even thinking that there might be a bear or a catamount in there, she pushed aside the brush curtain and stepped right in.

It took a moment for her eyes to adjust to the dim light. The cave wasn't very deep or tall; the top of her head was only centimetres from the ceiling. A smattering of late sunlight filtered through the opening and bounced against the walls, each beam something like the thin beam from her LED light, only instead of the steady white that that gave off, bits of this light glittered red, yellow, and orange.

The air was musty, filled with dried leaves and dirt ... and something else, something familiar. Coconut? Jules turned around and around in the small space. She wasn't imagining it.

Sam had given Sylvie a coconut candle for Christmas. That was it. That was what Jules smelled. The coconut candle. A glimmer of light flashed on the back wall. Ridges of dirt had been carved into the earthen walls like shelves, and each was lined with rocks.

On one of them, just above eye level, sat the candle, and right next to it was ... wait ... it couldn't be... Jules reached for her hand lens and clicked on the LED light. It was! It was the flamingo mug with the chip. Their mom's mug, the one that Sylvie had told Jules their dad must have moved because it must have made him too sad to see on the windowsill in the kitchen.

All those times that Sylvie took off running, running so that there was a big gap between them, she must have been running here! Sylvie had known about the Grotto all along and kept it a secret from her. And she had lied about the mug, too. She'd brought it here, along with the coconut candle.

Jules felt her cheeks burn with anger, felt her whole face light up. But almost as quickly she cooled down, because just then the little fox brushed up against her leg, like a cat who wanted attention. In the back of her mind she knew that this was a Do Not. *Do not touch a wild animal.* But here in the cave, the fox did not seem like a wild animal. She hardly even seemed like a fox. What was she? Jules didn't know. She reached down and ran her hand over the fox's coarse red fur. The fox didn't flinch.

"Thank you for bringing me here," Jules whispered. The fox sat down and wrapped her tail around her front paws.

Jules stepped forward until she stood directly in front of the wall of rocks. Cobwebs and dust covered many of them. Even with the light from her hand lens it was too dim to be able to tell what sort of rocks all of them were, but a few stood out: dolomite and kaolinite and muscovite schist and talc. The kind of rocks that caught light and held it. The kind of rocks that Jules herself prized in her collection.

The shelf with the flamingo mug and the candle was cleaner. Rocks lined it the same way that they lined Jules's shelves and windowsill at home. The rocks were arranged the way Jules would've arranged them.

But the other earthen shelves were covered with dust and dirt and cobwebs. Those rocks had been there for a long, long time. She reached out to touch one, but then withdrew her hand. Someone, long ago, someone she didn't know and never would, had left that rock in honour of someone important. Someone like Zeke. Someone like her mother. Jules felt a buzz run through her. *That* was why Sylvie had brought the mug! To honour their mother!

Jules pulled the rock her dad had given her, the verde antique rock, from her pocket. She felt its heft in her hand as memories, a stream of them, flooded through her. Memories of Sylvie. Sylvie snaking her forefinger across the blanket, Sylvie making snow families, Sylvie telling her about their mother, how Mom liked black licorice, never red. She loved to sing but had a terrible voice. She always won at marbles.

That was when Jules understood why Sylvie had never told her about this place. She had needed it for herself. Sylvie had worked so hard to keep their mother's memory alive for Jules;

but here, in this hidden place, she didn't have to work at all. Instead she could just be alone with her own memories. In this place she didn't have to share anything at all, not even with Jules.

The fox remained sitting and waited quietly while Jules took it all in. Jules began to say the names of the rocks out loud: "Granite, limestone, marble" … names that Sylvie probably wouldn't know. Sylvie knew a lot about a lot of things, but she didn't know everything. Jules was the one who had the eye for rocks, who knew one from another and where they were found in Vermont and New Hampshire and lots of other places. After all, she had been the supplier of wish rocks.

And in the midst of all the rocks, there was the flamingo mug. Jules slipped the serpentine back into her pocket and lifted the mug off the shelf as carefully as she had ever lifted anything in her life. Her mother's mug.

Wait. There was something inside it.

Jules shook it. A rock, of course. And something else, too, poking out just above the rim. A waterproof marker. It took Jules a second, but then she realized: Sylvie had also come here to write her wish rocks. Her burning wishes, every one of which was the same: *To run faster, so that...*

Jules looked down at the fox, still so patient there on the dusty dirt floor.

"So that WHAT, though?"

Jules sighed. She plucked the waterproof marker out of the mug and then she shook the piece of limestone out onto her palm. It was a perfect wish rock, a little bigger than a half-dollar and nearly flat on one side, a good surface for writing on.

But something was already written on it. Jules held it under her LED light. *To run faster.* Of course. Sylvie's one wish. It was strange and painful to see it, Sylvie's wish in Sylvie's handwriting without Sylvie in the world any more.

"It's not fair," she said to the fox. The same thing she had said to Sam. There wasn't any anger in her today, though. Only sadness. And a kind of wonder, that Sylvie had kept this secret from them all. She turned the rock over, to hide her sister's wish. But there were words on the other side too.

To keep Jules safe.

To keep
Jules safe

35

Jules stared at the words. "To keep me safe?" she said aloud. "What does that mean?"

She flipped the rock over, then back. *To run faster, to keep Jules safe.*

The other rocks on the flamingo mug shelf all had writing on them too, she saw now. She picked up the first one, a piece of granite. On the front side, facing out, was the familiar wish: *To run faster.* But on the back?

To keep Dad safe.

Now Jules picked up the third and fourth and fifth and sixth rocks, flipping from the front to the back. They were all the same — *To run faster* on the front, and either *To keep Dad safe* or *To keep Jules safe* on the back. She flipped each rock on the shelf, twenty of them, thirty, she didn't keep count. All the same.

She sank to her knees. The fox hadn't moved, not even one millimetre. She just sat back quietly, as if she were waiting for Jules to say something or do something.

"Keep us safe from what?" Jules said to her, as if the fox might know. "And how? By running faster? That doesn't make any sense."

But one more memory rose up inside her, a memory of a morning long ago, soon after their mom had died, when Dad had given them each a cup of hot chocolate. He had put it in their Peter Rabbit double-handled cups. They were still in their pyjamas and Dad was making breakfast. But Sylvie wasn't happy. She stood in front of Dad, arms crossed, feet planted.

237

"The mug," she said. Sylvie wanted her hot chocolate in their mom's flamingo mug.

Dad had argued with her. "Sylvie," he told her, "it's too heavy for you." But she insisted. Jules remembered it, she remembered her dad sighing and then finally setting the mug on the table in front of Sylvie. "Be careful," he told her, "this was your mom's favourite mug." Jules knew that was true. She could just see her mom, standing at the kitchen window with the mug in her hand.

But as soon as Sylvie lifted the mug to her mouth, it slipped out of her hand and tumbled to the floor. Hot chocolate sloshed onto the rug beneath the table, tiny marshmallows clinging to the braids while the chocolate soaked in.

Jules remembered Sylvie's horrified face, the way she burst into tears, the way Dad told her over and over, "Honey, it's OK. The mug was too big for you." He set it on the table and they all saw the broken spot on the rim, a bright white chip.

Sylvie pushed the mug away from her, then put her arms on the table and buried her face in them.

"It's OK, baby. It's OK." Dad said it over and over. But for Sylvie, it wasn't OK. Jules didn't say anything. All she could do was sit there at the table, the hot chocolate soaking into the rug and Sylvie crying so hard, harder than ever.

Daddy had reached across the wet rug and lifted Sylvie out of her chair and into his arms, and Sylvie, her face a mess of tears and snot, just kept repeating over and over, "Daddy, I ran as fast as I could."

"Of course you did, Sylvie. You ran so fast. Nobody could have run faster." Jules had to keep wiping her own face, crying because Sylvie was crying.

At last Sylvie had said, "Next time I'll run faster."

There in the Grotto, Jules doubled over as if someone had taken her rock hammer and swung it right into her stomach.

Next time I'll run faster.

"Oh, Sylvie," Jules said. "Sylvie." At last she knew the end of the sentence ... so that...

Her mother had fallen, the jar of mustard had cracked open. And ever since, Sylvie had run fast. *As fast as the jet stream. As fast as a stingray. As fast as a fireball.* She was the fastest girl at Hobbston School. She ran so fast that she had to grab on to things to slow herself down – the porch rail, tree branches – she even grabbed on to Jules, sometimes pulling them both over. But that morning, that morning of new snow, with the banks of the river covered in ice, there had been nothing to slow her pace at the edge of the Slip, nothing for her to grab on to. No porch rail, no tree branch, no Jules.

No Mom.

Jules stood up now, the flamingo mug tight in her hands.

"She didn't want it ever to happen again," she

said slowly, her voice cracking, to the fox. "If it ever did, she was going to be ready."

Her sister's one burning wish had been to keep Jules and Dad safe. She had felt responsible for their mother's death. Ever since that terrible day, the day the mustard jar burst open at the foot of the steps, Sylvie had been convinced that if she had run faster their mom might still be alive. But it had been Sylvie who died. She had run too fast.

Jules reached into her pocket and pulled out the serpentine rock. She had brought it with her to honour Sylvie. Now it burned in the palm of her hand, and Jules knew that if she threw it into the Slip it would shine up from the bottom like a shooting star. And Jules also knew this: she needed to break the rules just one last time. One very last time. She would take this rock to the Slip and throw it in the water. For Sylvie.

And for me, too, Jules thought.

Because as of this minute, she had a brand-new burning wish. She picked up the waterproof marker and wrote it down on the verde green serpentine:

That Sylvie knows how much I love her.

How that could ever be, Jules didn't know. But if there were any way for a message to reach her sister, wherever she was, *if* she was, then a wish rock wished on here in the Grotto and thrown into the Slip seemed like the way to do it. She put the flamingo mug and the pen back up on the shelf. They had been safe here in the Grotto, and they would still be safe.

Maybe this was what her sister had left behind for her, a place where she could come to remember their mother. A place to think about her sister. Jules slid the new wish rock into her pocket and stepped out of the cave. At her heels, one small red fox.

36

Senna knew that something was about to happen even though she didn't know what it was. Jules was walking towards the river, towards the Disappearance.

Never, her mother had told her. *Never go to the Disappearance.*

But she could tell that Jules was heading in that direction. And Senna had to follow her, to stop her. She had led Jules to the cave because she thought the Someone, the woman with the red-brown hair, might greet them together. But the woman hadn't come.

Now Jules picked up her pace. Senna hurried to keep up.

Danger. Run faster, little Senna.

Yes. The woman had told her those words. Now they filled her ears. Now they streamed along her back. Now they pushed her.

Faster. Run faster.

And then, from a distance, *Kapow!* The sound of a rifle split the darkening air.

37

If Jules's ears had been as keen as Senna's she might have heard the sound of the gun, but they weren't. All she heard as she moved along the path were her own beating footsteps and the growing sound of the river. The wish rock was deep inside Jules's pocket and her mother's headband was looped around her wrist. She had no idea how long she had been in the Grotto. What she did know was that by now, she was sure, her father would be home and looking for her. He would know right away that she had crossed the invisible line.

She figured he would be angrier than she'd ever seen him. And scared. She was scared too. As she ran, she promised him, *I'll never break a Do Not again.* The sun hid behind a cloud, and the woods took on a deeper shade of grey. She thought she heard a new noise. Footsteps. Were there footsteps over there, to her left?

She looked to both sides to see if she could spot the fox, but she had disappeared. There was no sign of her. Maybe the fox wasn't real after all. Maybe, Jules thought, she had imagined her. She stopped for just a moment, to see if there was any sign of her. Nothing. But then … footsteps?

Maybe the bear, she reminded herself. He was a sneaky thing, still lurking around Archer's Sheep Farm across the river and being a nuisance throughout the entire area.

And the catamount, too. Why she didn't feel more afraid, knowing that the giant cat had been in these woods, she didn't know. Maybe the cat wasn't real either. But hadn't she seen the paw print?

The woods grew dimmer. Jules's senses went on high alert. She took a deep breath and the damp aroma of mushrooms filled her nostrils; another breath, and the sweet leaves of sugar maple.

Her eyesight felt sharper. She noticed the odd shapes of sunlight that splashed onto the ground like puzzle pieces, fading fast, growing smaller in the waning day. With her fingertips she felt the smooth ridge of the serpentine rock she carried in her pocket. It would be the last one. She would never go to the Slip again after this.

She listened hard for footsteps, but there were only her own, hurrying along. That and the river, that was all the sound there was ... until it wasn't. It began with a rustling. She cocked her ears. The sound stopped. She sped up, nearly running now, listening. The light was falling too fast to linger. She couldn't stop now.

Hurry, she told herself. *Hurry.*

She ran. A patch of weak sunlight lit up the trail, casting a soft glow over the old rocks by the path. Sylvie's path. Sylvie had run on every path of the woods. Jules was running in Sylvie's footsteps. Fast. Sylvie was so fast. And suddenly it was as if Sylvie was there, everywhere, in the trees, in the pine needles that carpeted the ground, in the darkening air. The sound of the Whippoorwill rose up. Jules heard it before she saw it, and then she was there, right at the edge, watching the silvery water disappear beneath the rocky outcropping, vanishing. She stood there for a moment, and suddenly the woods were filled with sounds, sounds and more sounds –

the rush of the water
the whisper of the wind

the crash of a large animal running through the underbrush

Bear? Catamount? Human?

Voices?

Sam's voice, calling her, "Jules! Where are you?"

Elk beside him, his footfalls heavier, louder.

Mrs Harless, crying, "Jules!"

"JULES, JULES, JULES." Her father's voice.

And foxes, the high-pitched howls of foxes rang through the air...

38

K*apow!*

    Run! Run! Run!

At the sound of the gunshot Senna streaked away from Jules, leaping ahead of her and then darting through the woods towards the bear. She could smell him approaching, and he was crazy with pain. His ear. The bullet had grazed the very tip of his ear, and it was on fire. He pawed at it but that made it worse. He groaned and stumbled through the woods, seeking the path that led to the river. Water. Cold water to ease the pain.

The bear was moving fast now. It was too late to head him off away from Jules. Senna swerved back onto the path that led to the Disappearance, curving her narrow body just in time to avoid the big maple that marked the trail's beginning.

Never, her mother had said, in the language of fox.

Run faster, the Someone said, in the language of Kennen.

Far behind her, halfway across the field, rose the howl of a fox.

Older Brother was sounding the alarm. *BEAR. SENNA.* As Senna ran she scented her family. Mother, Father, Younger Brother, rising to their feet and emerging from the hollow. Now her mother began to bark, a vixen's cry of warning to her young. She was calling her daughter home to her, home to the hollow. Home.

But Senna ran on. This was what she was supposed to do.

The blood of her ancestors ran swiftly through her slender body and her heart pounded. It was dusk now, the last rays of the sun slanting across the fields. A new scent.

Catamount.

The huge cat had uncoiled himself from the branches of the tree near the cave and was slinking his way to the river, metres from Sam and Elk.

Bear.

Young and electrified with pain from his wound, the bear had reached the river. He was at the Disappearance now, searching for water, for something to take away the fire in his ear. He could taste his own blood. He rose to his hind feet and pawed at the rocks on the ledge. Water.

He was not alone. Senna scented the farmer waiting, silent and still at the edge of the pines. Now he raised his rifle to his shoulder. Now his hands tightened their grip and his finger tensed on the trigger. He would finish the job he had started.

Run! Faster!

Jules was nearing the Disappearance. Senna had to run faster than she ever had, so fast...

"Jules!"

"Jules!"

"Jules!"

The foxes howled for Senna: Mother, Father, Younger Brother and Older Brother, his voice the loudest of all. *Come back. Come back. Come back.*

"Jules," cried the man. "Come back! Bear. Hunter." His voice gave out but he kept running, almost to the river, almost to where Jules stood now at the Disappearance, where the tumbling water hid the sound of her father's voice, hid the sound of the foxes, hid everything.

Senna got there first. She crouched in the low bushes next to Jules, who was almost invisible in the near darkness. Blood pounded through

Senna's body, the fur rose high on the back of her neck.

The young bear blundered to the edge of the water next to Jules, who turned in shock at the sight of him. In that moment, the hunter pulled the trigger.

And from the bushes Senna sprang.

39

Falling.

She was falling.

Senna was falling, falling.

First there was snow. The white wisps were cold and feathery. Snowflakes gathered fast and light around her falling body. Faces hovered above her, looking down. Jules and Dad and Sam and Elk. The hidden catamount. All of them. The hunter was running towards them, shouting in horror. The bear was gone, fumbling into the woods, his ear on fire.

Far across the field the sound of crying foxes rose in the air.

Senna fell and fell and fell.

Jules's eyes met hers as she fell from the above world into the world between. The girl's eyes were wide and full of something – what? Senna looked into them and waited as she fell, waited for her Kennen senses to tell her what Jules was feeling.

But then the grey-green bars, the ones that had hovered all around her since she was born into this world, shifted from grey and green into a dozen other colours, blue, red, purple, yellow ... and then vanished in the cool, white air.

It was then that Senna knew she was leaving.

She would not be back.

She was leaving it behind, the above world with its brown earth that gave beneath her paws, the above world with its meadow voles and mice, its slanting sun and tall waving grass and hidden animal trails. She was leaving behind the rushing river and the clouds massing above the far ridge line. She was leaving behind her family: Younger Brother and Father and Mother. She was leaving behind Older Brother.

Older Brother.

For one long moment then she fought, her paws scrabbling against the fast and falling white snowflakes. She fought to return to the above world – *run, run* – so that she could crawl into the dugout, press herself against Older Brother's warmth, his tawny fur, his solid calm.

Brother.

She struggled hard in that moment. Even as she was disappearing, the memory of those early weeks with her brother came flooding through her – *Pounce! Bat bat bat.* Rolling and tumbling and wrestling on the soft, fragrant grass in that new world.

But the moment passed, and then it was gone.

Too late. Too late.

Older Brother was in the above world now, and she was falling. She released her hold on that world. She let herself fall. And she looked down.

Far below, Senna saw her: the Someone. The woman with the red-brown hair, her arms outstretched. Her head was tilted back and she was looking up, far up, at Senna. Their eyes met and held. The above world was gone now, and the woman held out her arms. She did not turn away. Love washed over Senna in a wave. At last!

Then her fall slowed. Snowflakes clung to her copper fur. New snow. There was a look in the woman's eyes as she waited, her arms held up and open. Senna knew that look. She had seen it before. This Someone had been waiting for her.

Now the woman caught her and held her in her arms, arms that Senna had missed for such a long, long time.

My little girl, she said. *My baby.*
Then she called her by name.
Sylvie.

40

The fox fell.

She fell from the sky, a red comet blazing back to earth.

Maybe you turn into wind.

Maybe you turn into stars.

Maybe you go to another world.

Maybe you turn into a fox. And you run and run and run, faster than a torpedo, faster than the sound of light, faster than a speeding bullet.

You run faster so that you can keep the ones you love most safe.

41

Dad said it was coincidence, a freakish stroke of luck that had saved her life.

"That fox came out of nowhere," Sam said.

Elk and Mrs Harless didn't say anything, but Jules saw him put his arms around Mrs Harless, and she watched them hold on tight to each other. Mr Archer kept apologizing, *I'm so sorry, I'm so sorry, I should never have gone after that bear, I am so sorry,* his words tumbling out, over and over, like the water that kept tumbling over the rocks into the Slip. It would tumble that way for ever.

Later that night, after they had all gathered in the Sherman kitchen, sat around the table and hashed through it again and again, everyone left and it was just Jules and her dad. "A freak coincidence," he said again. "A stroke of luck. Thank God you're OK, Juley-Jules."

Then he had gone to sit in the living room by himself, his head bowed and his hands laced together.

But Jules knew: the fox had saved her life. And maybe someday she would tell Dad or Sam or Elk or all of them how she knew it. But not yet. Not now.

Instead she spread her rock collection out on Sylvie's bed and began sorting. First into the three categories of rocks: igneous, sedimentary and metamorphic. Then by size within each category. Then into vertical rows, horizontal rows and circles. She whispered their names aloud as she worked. "Marble. Slate. Schist. Quartzite.

Sandstone. Flint. Dolomite. Agate."

Tomorrow she would give the agates back to Elk and tell him where the Grotto waited. She would miss them, so similar, but she knew that she had only kept them safe. They belonged to Elk ... and Zeke. She picked up the chunk of marble, the one that Sylvie had given her for her birthday. It was her favourite, warm to the touch, smooth on one side and coarse on the other. *Like Sylvie,* she thought.

This was the one she would take to the Grotto in honour of the fox. She thought Sylvie would agree. A shiver of sadness went through her because she wasn't going to see the fox ever again. Sadness mixed with gratitude because the little fox was the reason she was here, in her bedroom, still alive.

Dad knocked softly on the door.

"Juley-Jules?"

"It's open," she said, and he came in and

sat down at the foot of the bed, careful not to disturb the rocks.

"I'm never going to the Slip again," she said, in case he was about to bring it up, about to tell her it was forbidden. He started to say something, but stopped. Maybe because he could hear how flat and final her voice was.

The serpentine stone was next to his knee. He picked it up and tossed it from hand to hand, then stopped to read the message.

That Sylvie knows how much I love her.

"Oh, Jules."

Dad was here. Jules was here. And both of them were safe.

Jules crawled across the rocks, messing them all up, their edges sharp beneath her knees. She didn't care. She put her arms around her dad, and they sat that way for a long time, a quiet Sherman Galaxy of two, rocks tumbling on the blanket beneath them.

42

The fox made his way through the dark woods alone. At one point he half turned and breathed deeply of the air behind him, scenting the hollow, the brush pile from where he had risen. Mother, Father, Younger Brother: all asleep. Even his mother, who had cried for hours. Who had not stopped shrieking her vixen's cry of alarm even after the shot exploded across the Disappearance, even after the leaping streak of red-brown fur had fallen into the tumbling water that bore her body down.

Here he was now, at the Disappearance. The

river was urgent, its splashing tumble turned to a low roar as it gathered speed just before the earth swallowed it up. The fox carried the memory of his sister's bright eyes, the way she would tilt her head at him. He carried the memory of the early days, when together they had rolled and tumbled and wrestled together, growling and playing and batting each other with their paws.

The above world had been new to them then. The sun with its light and warmth, the tall waving grass, the smell of pine and thunderclouds and meadow creatures hidden in their burrows.

Senna.

Senna, returning to the dugout in the late evening, pressing herself against his back. His sister, leading him through the woods to the old cave. To the oxbow, where gunshots had exploded the calm and the silent catamount watched from the nearby tree.

He breathed in deep and long and his body

filled with the scent of her fur, the memory of her warm and living body pressed to his back in the den.

Now he closed his eyes and then pointed his head up to the wide sky glittering and pulsing with light, stretching high above the world, and he keened his grief to that unknown world.

A fox. Crying for his sister.

ACKNOWLEDGEMENTS

From Kathi Appelt

A book never happens all by its lonesome, even one that has two brains and two hearts. I would like to thank the people who loaned their time and thoughts along the way, especially Rita Williams Garcia and Diane Linn. For her expertise with rocks and hammers, a huge thank you goes to Kerry Bowen White.

Just as the house was burning down, our agent, Holly McGhee, said, "I love this," and that made all the difference. And then Caitlyn Dlouhy, Editor of the World, brought her keen

green pencil to the page and helped us find our way through the rocky woods — and oh boy, were they rocky.

Thank you to my sweet husband, Ken, for staying in the car while I read and re-read multiple drafts of this story out loud, and thank you for not driving off a cliff in the process.

Finally, in a whole life, if we are lucky, a soul sister appears just when you need one the most. For me, that would be Alison. Ever since the two of us met in Nobel Hall one freezing night at Vermont College of Fine Arts to join that esteemed faculty, we've been starting and finishing each other's sentences. With this book, we jumped but she never let go.

From Alison McGhee

So much gratitude to the people and animals who inspired this book. To the fox that my daughter, Min and I witnessed in Wirth Park long ago;

the fox that my friend Nel and I were haunted by in the Florida Panhandle; and the fox I saw sauntering down Irving Avenue last year – thank you.

Thanks always to Holly McGhee, agent extraordinaire, for her insight, guidance and unshakeable support. Thanks to Devon O'Brien and Mary Rockcastle for their unforgettable reactions to an early draft reading at Hamline University years ago. Eternal thanks to Caitlyn Dlouhy, without whom this book (and many others) would not exist.

Finally, Sister Kathi, whom I met twelve years ago at Vermont College, was the one who first suggested that we write a book together. We began this novel not knowing anything except that it would be about two sisters and a fox. The four-year process of weekly back and forths was enormous work, and it was also magical. My gratitude, love and devotion to her know no bounds.

Kathi Appelt is the author of the bestselling *The Underneath*, which was awarded a Newbery Honor and was a National Book Award finalist, as well as National Book Award finalist *The True Blue Scouts of Sugar Man Swamp*, *Keeper* and many picture books. She has two grown-up children and lives with her husband in College Station, Texas, in the USA. Visit her at KathiAppelt.com.

Alison McGhee is *The New York Times* bestselling author of *Someday* and the critically acclaimed *Firefly Hollow* and *Shadow Baby*, as well as many other books for children, including the Bink and Gollie books, which she co-wrote with Kate DiCamillo. Alison lives in Minneapolis, Minnesota, USA, and you can visit her at AlisonMcGhee.com.